A Dark Foretoken

BOOKS BY MARC ALAN EDELHEIT

Chronicles of a Legionary Officer:
Book One: **Stiger's Tigers**
Book Two: **The Tiger**
Book Three: **The Tiger's Fate**
Book Four: **The Tiger's Time**
Book Five: **The Tiger's Wrath** (Coming 2019)

Tales of the Seventh:
Part One: **Stiger**
Part Two: **Fort Covenant**
Part Three: **A Dark Foretoken**
Part Four: **Thresh (Coming 2019/2020)**

The Karus Saga:
Book One: **Lost Legio IX**
Book Two: **Fortress of Radiance**
Book Three: (Coming 2019)

Way of the Legend:
Book One: **Reclaiming Honor** (Coming 2019)
Book Two: (Coming 2019)

A Dark Foretoken

Marc Alan Edelheit

This book is a work of fiction. Names, characters, places, and incidents are either the product of the author's imagination or are used fictitiously. Any resemblance to actual persons, living or dead, or to actual events or locales is entirely coincidental.

A Dark Foretoken: Tales of the Seventh, Part Three

First Edition

Copyright © 2019 by Marc Edelheit. All rights reserved, including the right to reproduce this book, or portions thereof, in any form. No part of this text may be reproduced, transmitted, downloaded, decompiled, reverse engineered, or stored in or introduced into any information storage and retrieval system, in any form or by any means, whether electronic or mechanical, without the express written permission of the author. The scanning, uploading, and distribution of this book via the Internet or via any other means without the permission of the publisher is illegal and punishable by law. Please purchase only authorized electronic editions and do not participate in or encourage electronic piracy of copyrighted materials.

I wish to thank my agent, Andrea Hurst, for her invaluable support and assistance. I would also like to thank my beta readers, who suffered through several early drafts. My betas: Jon Cockes, Nicolas Weiss, Melinda Vallem, Paul Klebaur, James Doak, David Cheever, Bruce Heaven, Erin Penny, April Faas, Rodney Gigone, Brandon Purcell, Tim Adams, Paul Bersoux, Phillip Broom, David Houston, Sheldon Levy, Michael Hetts, Walker Graham, Bill Schnippert, Jan McClintock, Jonathan Parkin, Spencer Morris, Jimmy McAfee, Rusty Juban, Marshall Clowers, Joel M. Rainey. I would also like to take a moment to thank my loving wife who sacrificed many an evening and weekend to allow me to work on my writing.

Editorial Assistance by Hannah Streetman, Audrey Mackaman

Cover Art by Piero Mng (Gianpiero Mangialardi)

Cover Formatting by Telemachus Press

Agented by Andrea Hurst & Associates

http://maenovels.com/

Author's note:

This story takes place after *Stiger: Tales of the Seventh, Part One*. You may wish to pick up that tale first and start from the beginning. It is available on Amazon Kindle, Audible and in Print.

The original name of this book was entitled *Eli*. Though Eli plays a strong role in this book, I made the decision to change the name, as I want to save the title *Eli* for a later, more pivotal book in this series. *A Dark Foretoken*, I think is a more fitting name for this story.

Tales of the Seventh began as an experiment... a way to give readers more Stiger while they waited for the Chronicles books. Released one chapter at a time for free on my website under the title of *The Interludes*, it was meant only to be a novella, but Part One quickly grew into a full-blown novel. It was an instant hit, with readers messaging me on Facebook and emailing questions and thoughts on what would happen next.

I fully intend to continue writing Tales of the Seventh books. They will always be on the shorter side and designed to be quick reads that will fill in Stiger and Eli's rich backstory.

You can visit my website to see concept art, learn about upcoming projects, or to sign up to my newsletter to get the latest updates.

Author's Website: http://maenovels.com/

Reviews keep me motivated and also help to drive sales. I make a point to read each and every one, so please continue to post them on Amazon, Goodreads, and Audible.

I hope you enjoy this book and would like to offer a sincere thank you for your purchase and support.

Best regards,

Marc Alan Edelheit, author and your tour guide to the worlds of Tannis and Istros

Chapter One

Stiger rubbed the back of his neck, massaging sore muscles. He leaned back on the stool and stretched his aching back. The light outside his tent had begun to die, and with it, the shadows had grown inside. The temperature had started to drop. He considered lighting a lamp, for he had several more hours of work yet ahead of him.

"Enough of this." Stiger pushed the company books and wax tablets aside. He was thoroughly disgusted. The amount of administrative work required by the legion was insane, even for a company that was nowhere near its allotted strength.

Not for the first time did he wonder who read all of the reports he was required to make. It was likely some sad bastard over at headquarters who had that unhappy duty. Stiger pitied the poor clerk, for each company was sending a like number of reports.

The legion had just held its biannual payday. The men were flush with their earnings. However, most of the payout went into their pensions. Stiger had spent the last two days reconciling these accounts. The task was made more complicated by the number of men lost, not only at Fort Covenant, but during the summer's campaign. Stiger was required to close out their pensions. The monies would be sent to their loved ones or next of kin. That was, if they had any. Should an heir not be found, the funds would be donated to a veterans' colony or some other worthy cause that the legion's general decided proper.

"I wouldn't be interrupting, would I?"

Stiger looked up to find Captain Lepidus of Tenth Company at the entrance flap. The captain had a hard face, almost as if it had been carved from marble, but just then it cracked. He was looking on Stiger with an amused, knowing smirk.

"No, you're not." Stiger expelled an unhappy breath. "I was just about to take a break. I will finish up later."

"I can tell you from experience it never finishes up," Lepidus said. "No matter how much you do, there is always more waiting to be done."

"Headquarters wants the men's pension accounts closed out," Stiger said. "They wanted them last week. I think that's how the clerk put it in the latest note."

"Headquarters is a demanding bunch," Lepidus said, stepping fully into the tent. He glanced around at the interior. Stiger was all about cleanliness and order. He felt that the example for the men began with him, and so he held himself to a higher standard.

"I'm beginning to discover that sad truth," Stiger said, eyeing the unfinished reports on his camp table.

"Hungry?"

"Very," Stiger said.

"Good, I'm heading over to the mess. Would you care to join me?"

"Gladly," Stiger said. "I've been trapped in this infernal tent all day doing work. It will be good to stretch my legs a little."

A spider climbed around the corner of the table and began moving slowly across the surface. Stiger squished it with the side of his hand.

"Don't like spiders?" Lepidus asked.

"No, not much."

Stiger stood and looked up at Lepidus as he wiped his hand with a small towel he used for cleaning his kit. Just weeks before, no other officer in the legion would have invited him to dine. Things had certainly changed. Where before he'd been an outcast, Stiger for the most part felt welcome, or at the least accepted, by much of the officer corps. Of course, there were those who still intensely disliked him. This was primarily due to his family history, but he tried not to let that bother him too much. With Lepidus, Stiger had earned his respect, and friendship.

Lepidus stepped back and out as Stiger exited the tent. The cool fall air was crisp. The evening before had seen flurries. It was clear winter was just around the corner, and Stiger was looking forward to the change in weather. It meant combat operations would come to a near end, barring patrols and the occasional skirmish.

Outside, Stiger glanced around. His tent was one of hundreds inside the legionary encampment. To his immediate right was the space allotted for his company. He found it depressing how few tents there were. After the ordeal at Fort Covenant, Seventh Company was all but a shadow of her former strength. Since they were short on men, the rest of the tents had not been pitched and remained stored away. Most of the space allotted to his company was unoccupied grass.

Stiger and Lepidus were neighbors, their tents pitched next to one another. To the left stretched out the Tenth's communal tents. Men were gathered around their fires, cleaning their kit. Stiger glanced back at his tent line. The men were nowhere to be seen. On Stiger's orders, Sergeant Tiro and Pazzullo had taken them out for a training march. They'd yet to return. That did not bother Stiger much.

Whenever the opportunity presented itself, he kept his boys busy, and that included lots of training.

"How are those recruits coming?" Lepidus asked as they stepped onto the street between tents and began walking in the direction of the mess. The ground was slightly muddy, yet another sign the fighting season was coming to a rapid end. "I understand that Colonel Aetius was able to get you ten more men."

"That he did. In total, I've gotten twenty fresh recruits over the last two weeks," Stiger said, "and another twenty-five auxiliaries. My current effective strength is up to sixty-five. I've ten wounded who likely won't return to full duties for gods know how long. Still, even with the new men, it's way short of the two hundred Seventh should have."

"Don't worry," Lepidus said. "Winter's almost here. The fighting season's already drawing to a close. Your company is not the only one short. At some point, the legion will receive large numbers of fresh recruits. We will have maybe four months to rest, recover, and train up the new kids."

A sergeant moving in the opposite direction saluted as he passed the two officers. Lepidus gave the sergeant a half-wave by way of reply. Then they were past. Lepidus looked over at Stiger.

"Before you know it, Seventh will be brought up to full strength, and then your administrative headaches will really begin."

"I find it hard to believe those headaches can get any worse," Stiger said.

"Oh, they can," Lepidus said.

The two officers dodged around a supply wagon that trundled by in the opposite direction. The teamster was chatting with someone behind the driver's box and had not seen them. The wagon's wheels kicked up flecks of muck and mud.

"How's Hollux doing?" Lepidus asked.

"Getting better each day. He's using a crutch now and is able to hobble around a bit," Stiger said. "That wound on his leg was a bad one, but the surgeon says it's healing nicely and he should make a full recovery. Hollux should be discharged from the hospital in a week or two and on light duty for the next two months."

"That's good to hear," Lepidus said.

"He's a solid man," Stiger said. "I believe he will make a good executive officer."

"I am told during the siege of Fort Covenant he acquitted himself quite well," Lepidus said.

"He did," Stiger confirmed. The lieutenant's auxiliary cohort had been virtually wiped out during the battle. "We both lost a lot of good men in that fort."

They turned a corner in the road and came to a large tent. All four sides of the tent had been rolled up and tied back, revealing dozens of tables. Though they were late to dinner, the officers' mess was still fairly crowded and noisy. Lanterns hung from the support poles or sat on tables. As the last of the day's sunlight disappeared behind the sea of trees that surrounded the legion's encampment, the lanterns gave the interior a yellowed light that Stiger found inviting.

The scent of beef stew carried on the air. Stiger's stomach rumbled. He was thrilled to be back in the comfort of the encampment, with no battles to fight for the time being. Just three weeks ago, Stiger and the Seventh had been inside Fort Covenant. Surrounded by a hostile Rivan army, they had helped to mount a desperate defense designed to hold long enough for Third Legion to arrive and relieve them. Faced with overwhelming numbers, the defenders had barely managed to hold.

At the end, with Third Legion nowhere in sight, the enemy had breached their defenses, pouring into the fort. It seemed they'd lost. Yet, on the cusp of victory, astonishingly, the enemy broke off their assault and withdrew, marching back to the north.

At the time, Stiger had not understood why. He'd subsequently learned General Treim had made a surprise move and, instead of marching to Fort Covenant's relief, had instead maneuvered Third Legion around, behind the enemy army, neatly cutting their supply line and communications. The move had caught the Rivan flatfooted. The battle that had followed had seen the Rivan badly beaten.

As they stepped inside the mess tent and into the lantern light, a number of officers called out greetings to Lepidus. A few gave Stiger a nod as he passed them by, but none hailed him a good evening. He had been accepted for the most part. That only meant his presence was tolerated. Stiger remained silent as they made their way through the tables to the back side of the tent. Food was laid out on a series of long tables. Lepidus and Stiger each picked up a bowl and got in line.

Since the battle, there had been a handful of minor skirmishes, but nothing more than that. The legion had settled down near the spot of the battle and had not moved since. Stiger couldn't understand why General Treim had not followed up his victory by actively pursuing the enemy and seeking their complete destruction. Stiger had heard the remains of the enemy army had occupied a position twenty miles distant, just north of the Cora'Tol Valley, and dug in. From rumors around the camp, they'd already been reinforced. Despite the victory, the inaction left a sour taste in Stiger's mouth.

It didn't take them long to make it through the line. Stiger ladled himself a generous helping of stew and took a bread roll, which was still slightly warm. He got himself a mug of water, while Lepidus took wine. The wine in the mess tent was poor quality and very watered down. Stiger despised the stuff. He followed Lepidus over to a long table with several officers clustered on the other end.

Stiger took a seat opposite Lepidus. The conversation at the other end of the table instantly stilled. One of the officers, a lieutenant by the name of Yanulus, threw his bread into his nearly empty bowl and made a disgusted sound that drew both Stiger's and Lepidus's attention. Glaring at Stiger, the lieutenant stood, as did his captain, who had been seated across from him. The other two officers came to their feet as well.

"Thank you for ruining my supper," Captain Corus said to Stiger. "Out of all the tables in this tent, you had to pick mine."

Corus spat on the ground.

Stiger put his hands on the rough wood of the tabletop and pushed himself to his feet, kicking back his stool. Lepidus reached across and grabbed Stiger's forearm, a clear warning in his eyes that said, *Don't do it, son.*

"Corus." Lepidus removed his hand and looked down the table at the other officers. "As a gentleman, you should show better manners."

"To him? A traitor's son?" Corus looked to Stiger, the disdain plain upon his pox-scarred face. "I guess you like to let others fight your battles for you."

Stiger saw red. He turned to fully face the other captain.

"Perhaps," Stiger said, clenching his fists, "you would care to back up those bold words?"

The entire tent stilled at that, all eyes upon them. Though dueling wasn't officially prohibited, there was an unwritten rule in Third Legion that such contests were frowned upon by the commanding general.

Corus looked abruptly uncertain. Nothing in the man's manner had changed, but Stiger sensed it in his eyes, which darted about the mess before returning to Stiger. Corus had served in the legions for five years. He was a veteran, like most of the other officers of the legion. Despite Corus's longer service, Stiger was certain he could take him in a fight, whether that be fists, knives, or swords. He suspected that Corus knew that as well. Stiger had changed a lot in the last few months, and he was finished taking shit from his peers. It started with the likes of Corus. He was drawing a line in the sand this day and everyone in the mess knew it.

"I'll not sully myself by playing with you, Stiger." Corus looked at his lieutenant. "Let's go."

The captain of Ninth Company started walking away, with the other officers who had been seated with him in tow.

"Next time you insult me, I will demand satisfaction," Stiger said to the man's back. It was not bravado, but a simple statement of fact. Stiger wanted things to be perfectly clear between them.

Corus stopped and glanced backward.

"I mean it, Corus," Stiger said. "Best take that to heart."

"If I choose to insult you," Corus said, "then I shall accept."

With that, Corus left the tent, his lieutenant and the two officers following. Stiger remained standing. His hands shook slightly with the anger of the moment. He glanced around at the other officers in the mess and then picked up his stool and sat back down. He stared at his bowl, no longer hungry. Conversation throughout the tent resumed a few heartbeats later. Any type of drama in camp was a welcome diversion, and Stiger had just given them one.

"That was unwise," Lepidus said finally. "In the last few weeks you've won over the respect of many and even impressed the general. You should be focused on keeping your head down and doing your duty. Trust me when I tell you Corus and those like him are not worth your time, energy, or your effort. You have the makings of a top-notch officer." Lepidus pointed a finger at him. "Don't throw away all you've done in a hotheaded moment. A duel is the last thing you should be seeking."

Stiger gave a nod but said nothing in return. He broke apart his hunk of bread and dipped it into the stew. He gave it a moment, allowing the bread to absorb as much stew as possible, and then took a bite. It wasn't the best he'd ever had, but Stiger hadn't eaten much this day and it certainly tasted good. Hunger frequently was the best cook.

"May I join you?"

Stiger looked up to find Eli standing at their table. The elf carried a bowl of stew. Over the last week, Stiger had hardly seen the ranger. Eli seemed to spend more time outside the encampment than in. What he did out there, Stiger had no idea. Tiro had told him it was an elf thing. Stiger's sergeant had felt Eli was just more comfortable in the forest than in the encampment.

"Gladly," Lepidus said, though Stiger noticed that as Eli sat down, the captain of the Tenth looked on the elf with something akin to wonder. That reaction seemed to be commonplace throughout the legion. Wherever Eli went, men and officers stopped what they were doing and turned their heads.

These days, it was a rare sight for elves to be out of their lands, let alone serving with the legions. The elves, though still tenuous allies with the empire, had withdrawn to their own lands. This made Eli's decision to attach himself to Stiger's company all the more surprising. There was no turning Eli away, either. General Triem and Colonel Aetius had made that plain, for it was their desire to see relations improve between the elven nations and the empire.

Stiger eyed the elf a moment. He had yet to figure out Eli's motivation, and that bothered him something fierce. Stiger took another bite of his bread, wondering what game the elf was playing.

Eli had not taken any bread for sopping the stew. Instead, he picked up the bowl and sipped directly from it. He placed the bowl back down on the table and grimaced.

"Clearly whoever made this needs to learn how to cook." Eli pushed the bowl away from him as if it were poison. "It's too salty, and the gods only know what kind of meat this was or, for that matter, even if it is fresh. I hesitate to call what was done to this stew *cooking*."

Lepidus almost choked on his stew. He swallowed with some difficulty and then began to laugh.

"Did I say something funny?" Eli asked, looking from Lepidus over to Stiger with a quizzical expression. "I had not intended to do so. I was being what I believe you call severe."

"I think you mean serious, right?" Stiger said.

"Yes, serious." Eli gave a pleased nod. "I was being what you call serious."

Lepidus began to laugh harder, pounding the table. Stiger even became amused, chuckling along with him. It was contagious, and soon the two of them were nearly doubled over in laughter. The tension of the encounter with

Corus and Yanulus had drained away. Several officers at the nearest table looked over.

"Eli, I think you will fit in just fine with the legions," Lepidus said as he recovered and caught his breath. He took a bite of his bread and then shook it at Eli. "Yes, you will fit in just fine."

"He served with Tiro," Stiger said.

"You did?" Lepidus said, becoming serious. "In the Wilds?"

Eli gave a nod.

"I understand that was a difficult campaign," Lepidus said.

"It was," Eli said quietly. "Sadly, many of my people were lost. The Tainen were a terrible foe to both our peoples. It is good they have been crushed, their temples torn down, and what remains of their people scattered to the winds."

An uncomfortable silence returned to the table. Lepidus broke it. "Well then, since you've served with us before, this kind of fare is something you must have been exposed to?"

"That is true," Eli said in a ho-hum sort of manner. "A cousin of mine took it upon himself to teach your cooks how to better prepare food and make it somewhat, shall we say, tastier. It appears his efforts were wasted."

"The campaign in the Wilds was, what… ten years ago?" Lepidus said. "I would hazard most legionary cooks from that time have long since retired and moved on."

"I'd hoped they had at least passed along the knowledge and skill my cousin imparted," Eli said. "It is distressing to learn that his efforts were wasted."

"Are you serious?" Stiger asked Eli. He got the feeling that the elf wasn't quite as sincere as he was making himself out to be.

"Only half so," Eli said with a shrug.

Lepidus grinned, dipped his bread into his stew, and swirled it around a bit. "You had me there for a moment."

Eli picked up his bowl and took another generous sip, slurping as he did. He then set the wooden bowl back down on the table. He wiped his mouth carefully with a small, delicate white cloth he produced from his tunic.

"I am thinking," Lepidus said, shaking his sodden bread roll in Stiger's direction now. Droplets of juice from the stew fell onto the wooden table. "You, son, are in for an interesting time with this elf."

"You have that wrong," Eli said to Lepidus. "It is I who am in for an interesting time of it."

Stiger looked from Lepidus to Eli. "I think I've had enough excitement to last me a while. I'd like a quiet winter. Is that too much to ask?"

"No," Lepidus said, his eyes upon the elf. There was a shrewd look upon the captain's face. "I think I have the right of it. Eli, you are going to drive him absolutely crazy."

"Perhaps," Eli said with a glance over at Stiger. "It depends on how boring things get."

Stiger did not like the sound of that. He still felt uncomfortable in the elf's presence and even more so that Eli had chosen to attach himself to Stiger's company. Since they had returned, the Seventh had been the talk of the legion, not only for what they had done at Fort Covenant, but also because of Eli. With Stiger's family reputation in tatters, he did not need any more attention. All he desired to do was serve his empire and god faithfully.

"If I recall correctly, elves are well-known for their unique sense of humor," Lepidus said. "Isn't that so?"

"I wouldn't know about that," Eli said with a straight face as his eyes slid over to Stiger and then back to Lepidus. "However, upon occasion I like to amuse myself on another's expense. If that could be considered humor...well, then, perhaps you heard correctly."

"Great," Stiger said. "Just bloody great."

Lepidus shot Stiger a knowing grin. "Better you than me, son."

"Excuse me, sir? Sorry to interrupt your dinner."

Stiger turned to see a legionary standing just behind him. Stiger recognized the man as being attached to headquarters. The legionary snapped to attention. He held out a dispatch. Wondering what bad news the dispatch contained, Stiger took it.

"Thank you," Stiger said. "You are dismissed."

"Yes, sir." The legionary saluted. He spared Eli a curious glance and then went on his way.

Stiger put his elbows on the table and tore open the dispatch, rapidly scanning its contents.

"It seems," Stiger said, looking up from the dispatch to Eli, "we are both wanted at headquarters."

Stiger took another bite of his bread and stood, pushing his stool back. He stuffed the dispatch into a tunic pocket. Eli stood as well.

"Does it say what for?" Lepidus asked.

"No," Stiger said. "Only that he and I are to report immediately."

"Maybe it's only about fresh recruits?" Lepidus said, though Stiger could tell the captain of the Tenth clearly thought otherwise.

Stiger glanced over at Eli and then back to Lepidus. If it was about recruits, they would not have called for Eli, too. There was a reason the two of them had been summoned to headquarters at such a late hour.

"Oh, before you go, I have a case of Venney," Lepidus said. "It was delivered this morning by special courier. I plan on opening a jar this evening and would be pleased if you both would join me for a taste. There's nothing like a fine jar of red and good company to help share it."

"That is very generous of you," Eli said with a glance over at Stiger. "We would be honored to join you."

Stiger looked over at Eli in surprise. He had been planning to accept Lepidus's invitation, but the fact that the elf had accepted for the both of them irritated Stiger slightly. He suspected that Eli knew this and had done it on purpose. Lepidus hadn't missed it either and wagged a finger at Eli.

"You are going to drive him to the brink of insanity," Lepidus said with a grin. "I can just tell."

"I am starting to think you might be right," Stiger said.

With that, he picked up his bowl and turned away. The more he thought on it, the stranger the dispatch seemed to him. He couldn't remember ever being summoned to headquarters at such an hour. He headed toward the table that held buckets for used bowls and plates. He placed his dirty plate in the buckets meant for used dishes and set out across the darkened camp with Eli at his side.

Chapter Two

Stiger came to a surprised halt as Livia stepped out of the headquarters tent, into the torchlight, and past the guard. She spotted Stiger and Eli. There was a moment's hesitation, almost a missed step, as she registered who it was. She flashed Stiger a dazzling smile and stepped up to them. Her body slave, a matronly woman in her forties, came to a halt a step behind Livia.

Stiger was extremely pleased to see Livia. It had been weeks since they'd set eyes upon one another and he felt a thrill at the unexpected encounter. The last time he'd seen her had been before he set out to retrieve Lieutenant Aggar from the Cora'Tol garrison. That mission culminated in Seventh Company ending up at Fort Covenant and had nearly cost Stiger his life.

"Ben," Livia said, a mischievous look in her eye. "So nice to run into you."

"When did you arrive?" Stiger asked, thinking she was a welcome sight for sore eyes. Her blonde hair, perfectly brushed, cascaded down her back. She wore a modest light-green dress, with a shawl draped around her shoulders. It was of the kind she could pull up and over her head should she wish shelter from the elements or prying eyes.

"Late this afternoon," Livia said.

"Livia," Stiger said, abruptly conscious of Eli at his side. The elf appeared curious and amused as he glanced between the two of them. "May I introduce Eli'Far."

"I've had the pleasure of making his acquaintance," Livia said, giving Eli a warm smile. "He and I are old friends."

"You have? You are?" Stiger was surprised by that, but then realized he should not have been. Eli had been with the general for weeks before he had attached himself to Stiger's company. It was only natural that they should have crossed paths.

"Eli," Livia said, extending her hand to him.

Eli took a graceful step toward her, as if at the emperor's court. With one hand held behind his back, he leaned forward and took the offered hand, brushing it with his lips in a gentle kiss. He looked up at Livia and returned her smile with one of his own before he straightened. "A pleasure, as always, my dear."

He held her hand a moment more before releasing it.

Stiger felt an intense stab of jealousy. Livia flushed slightly, her gaze lingering on Eli. Stiger realized his mouth was hanging open stupidly. He clamped it shut, just as she returned her attention to him. Livia flashed him another smile. In the darkness, lit only by torchlight, it was as if the sun had suddenly risen in all its glory.

"Ben, when you are able to pry yourself away from your duties," Livia said, "perhaps we can find time to go for a walk or maybe even a ride? Get to know each other once again, if you will. It's been too long."

"I would like that very much," Stiger said. "Would you have time tomorrow afternoon?"

"I do, yes," Livia said with a slight pout. "Sadly, you do not."

"I don't understand." Stiger glanced over at Eli. Then it hit him. He was being sent out on a mission of some kind, and she knew.

"It will have to wait," Livia said, lowering her voice in a conspiratorial manner and making a show of looking around for listening ears. She leaned close to Stiger and Eli. "I'm not supposed to know, but my father has a job for you both."

"Oh?" Stiger asked curiously. He wondered how dangerous this job would be, particularly considering they had been called to headquarters after hours.

"Well," Livia said with a light laugh that sounded quite pleasant to Stiger's ears, "I won't spoil the fun for my father. You should be gone no more than a few weeks. With any luck, you will be back before the first snows. Then we can spend some time together. I do so miss your company, Ben."

She stepped up to him and planted a peck on his cheek. As she pulled away, she gave Stiger a quick wink, then nodded to her slave and turned to leave. Eli stepped aside to allow her passage between them and inclined his head as she passed. Her perfume, a lavender of some kind, remained on the air after her passage. Stiger found it alluring. They both turned and watched Livia as she moved off into the darkness, her slave following along behind.

"I do believe she likes you," Eli said. He shot Stiger a wink, imitating Livia.

"What gave you that idea?" Stiger asked with an unhappy frown.

"I wonder, maybe the kiss on your cheek?" Eli flashed him a closed-mouth grin. "Or perhaps, the 'I do so miss your company, Ben.' It was rather obvious, don't you think? You humans show too much emotion when it comes to, how you say, devotion?"

Stiger shot Eli an unhappy look. "Love?"

"Yes," Eli said, pleased. "That is the word. You are a lucky man, I think." Eli glanced toward the headquarters tent. "I wonder, do you think her father knows?"

"By the gods, I hope not." Stiger started forward without another word. The headquarters guard snapped to attention as Stiger made his way into the administrative tent with Eli following. He understood the guards had just witnessed everything that had passed between him and Livia. He could well imagine the rumors that would be making their way around camp come morning. It would only be a matter of time until the general discovered his daughter's flirtations with Stiger. He was not looking forward to that day.

Putting the guard and the inevitable rumors from his mind, Stiger found the headquarters tent well lit, with lanterns hanging from support poles. Several tallow candles burned on tables too, adding to the usable light. The tent smelled strongly of tallow, lamp oil, ink, waterproofed canvas, and smoke from a brazier that had been lit.

Though the hour was late, there were still six clerks bent over tables, reading reports or scribbling away with styluses on wax tablets or scratching in ink on vellum. The tent hummed with activity. Four messengers were standing by on the far side of the tent, patiently waiting to be called.

One of the clerks looked up as Stiger moved farther into the tent. The man had a busy air about him and, from his expression, appeared to resent the intrusion upon his work.

"May I help you, sir?" the clerk asked, standing. Gone was the resentful look. He approached Stiger with a carefully schooled expression of equanimity. Stiger knew him to be Lenovus, the chief clerk. Lenovus was a skinny, balding man in his early thirties with ink-stained hands. Though he was just a freedman, it was rumored the general held him in high esteem and had brought him all the way from the capital.

"Captain Stiger, reporting as ordered," Stiger said, certain Lenovus knew exactly who he was and why he was here.

"Ah, yes," the clerk said with a slight scowl. "You were sent for over an hour ago, sir."

"I came straight away, as soon as I received the summons," Stiger said, wondering if the clerk was playing a game. "I did not dally, if that is your meaning."

"Yes, sir," Lenovus said in a tone that was carefully neutral. "Please wait here. I will let the general know you have arrived."

"Thank you," Stiger said.

The clerk moved over to the adjacent tent that served as the general's office. That tent came right up to the edge of the administrative tent. The side of the general's tent, broken only by a canvas flap, functioned as a partition to give the general some privacy. Lenovus pulled back the flap and held it aside, poking his head inside.

"Excuse me, sir," Lenovus said.

"What is it?" came the general's deep voice.

"Captain Stiger and the elven ranger Eli'Far to see you, sir."

"It's about time," Treim said, in a tone that sounded far from pleased. "Send him right in."

The clerk stood aside. He held back the flap and motioned for them to enter.

Stiger led the way into the tent. He found the general standing before a large table. Colonel Aetius was there with him. Both were staring intently at a map laid out on the table. Rocks had been placed along the edges of the map to hold the corners down. Wooden markers were positioned about the map.

General Treim looked up with an expression that spoke of disapproval. It was the kind of look a father might give a child. The general was a tall man, with short-cropped brown hair, a long face, and a jaw that looked as if it had been chiseled from stone. The general's nose was slightly hooked, and his lips were drawn into a thin line. Treim's eyes were piercing and spoke of a deep intelligence. Stiger noted the dark bags that hung under the general's eyes. He looked like a man starved of sleep, with the weight of the world on his shoulders.

Stiger stepped forward. He snapped to attention and saluted, fist to chest, as the clerk let the tent flap fall back into place.

"Reporting as ordered, sir," Stiger said and then made sure to add, "I came just as soon as I received the summons, sir."

Treim gave a nod and straightened, crossing his arms. He took a long moment to study Stiger and Eli. Stiger felt uncomfortable under the unexpected scrutiny. The general uncrossed his arms and placed his hands back on the table, leaning forward to study the map. Stiger remained where he was, standing at attention.

"That was some fine work at Fort Covenant," Treim said in a grudging tone, glancing up from the map. "Prefect Merritt has good things to say about you, son. I've known Merritt for more than twenty years. He's never been one to speak very highly of others, unless they've impressed him. You seem to have done that."

"Yes, sir," Stiger said, keeping his expression neutral. "I did nothing other than what I thought was my duty."

"So it seems," Treim said, "and even doing that you impressed Colonel Aetius as well." Treim threw a glance over to the colonel. "That is a hard thing to do."

"The captain is a credit to the legion," Aetius said.

Stiger was uncomfortable with the unexpected praise, especially in light of his family's reputation.

"You've gotten my attention, too," Treim said, tone turning unhappy. "However, you failed in your mission. Lieutenant Aggar escaped you."

"Yes, sir," Stiger said, stiffly. He felt sore about that. Stiger had been sent to fetch Aggar and, at the time, had no idea why other than to bring him back to the general. Stiger had learned later that the lieutenant was suspected of selling information to the enemy. In the end, Aggar had turned out to be a traitor in the service of the Rivan.

"That was not Stiger's fault," Aetius said to Treim. "Merritt confirmed as much."

"No," Treim said and let out a heavy breath. "You are quite correct. It was that fool Declin's fault. I thought by getting that arrogant ass promoted to tribune and assigning him to an out-of-the-way command, I could keep him from causing too much trouble." The general paused and looked over at Stiger. "It seems I was wrong. So, in the end, the responsibility for Aggar's escape is mine alone. I do not hold that against you, Captain."

Stiger didn't quite know what to say to that, so he kept his mouth shut.

"And you?" The general abruptly turned his attention onto Eli, acknowledging the elf's presence for the first time. "You survived the ordeal at Covenant. From what Aetius tells me, it was a close thing. The captain here seems to attract all kinds of trouble, and not the good kind, either. There are safer assignments than tagging along with him."

"I assume there are," Eli said with a look over at Stiger.

"Are you still intent on sticking with Captain Stiger and his company?"

"I am," Eli said. "I cannot think of a better officer in the legion with whom to attach myself as...shall we say, an observer for my people."

The general grunted, regarding Eli a long moment before turning his gaze back on Stiger. "I have a job for the two of you."

General Treim motioned Stiger and Eli forward to the table and the map.

"This is our position here, nearly on the border of the Forests of Abath and Rivan territory." The general pointed at the map. "The forests are a dense tangle of unmapped woodlands that make the Wilds appear tame by comparison. To the north of us, occupying the Cora'Tol Valley, is an enemy army numbering at least twenty thousand. They are freshly reinforced, but still recovering from the beating we gave them. To the west"—the general slid his hand across the map and tapped a position along a north-south road—"are the three legions we marched north with, the Second, Eighth, and Fourteenth. They are facing the main body of the enemy, numbering somewhere around sixty thousand in total strength. As you know, after we forced a crossing of the river, our legion was put in reserve to recover and protect the army's communications. The other three legions pushed farther north and pursued the enemy deeper into their territory. What you might not know is that a series of battles between our legions and the main enemy army were fought over the last few weeks. No advantage was gained by either side, other than to see a great effusion of blood for all involved." Treim looked up at Stiger. "Are you with me so far?"

"Yes, sir," Stiger said. He had heard talk of such action, but nothing definitive. It was good to know the tactical situation and not have to piece it together from rumor or secondhand knowledge.

"Good," Treim said, "for had you not discovered the enemy's intention to flank our drive into Rivan territory, we would be looking at a very different tactical and strategic picture."

Stiger said nothing.

The general glanced up briefly from the map and their eyes met.

"That was some damn fine intelligence you came across that alerted us to the enemy's intentions." Treim looked back down and swung his finger back to Third Legion's position, marked by a small block of wood, and then farther to the east, to the Inland Sea. "There is a city by the name of Thresh, about here." The general tapped the map, which did not show the city in question. Treim tapped the same spot for emphasis.

"I've heard of it, sir," Stiger said. "I've never had the pleasure of visiting, but if I recall, Thresh is an island city on the northern end of the sea. For the most part, the empire's ignored them."

"Not willingly," Treim said.

"One of the reasons they've avoided being swallowed up by us is that King Kronen of Thresh has a powerful navy," Aetius said. "The king's fleet is numerous, experienced, and quite capable." Aetius paused and pointed at the map. "The northern end of the sea is effectively his own personal lake. From time to time the empire has considered ending Thresh's neutrality and taking the city by force. However, any potential rewards gained from seizing the city would be far outweighed by the costs. Hence the real reason Thresh remains an independent power."

"Let's be honest," Treim said. "Even if the senate approved the expenditure needed, any attempt to overcome Thresh's navy would be questionable at best."

"It would be a difficult venture," Aetius conceded. "With the war against the Rivan already eating up the treasury, the senate is unlikely to approve such an effort unless forced to."

"They are not the problem," Treim said, moving his hand to the country above the Inland Sea. "Castol Mallara is our problem. It is rumored they are about to enter into an alliance with the Rivan. And by rumored, I mean our spies have confirmed this intelligence as fact. It is not yet public knowledge."

"They are a long way from us, sir," Stiger pointed out.

"Correct," the general said. "To get to us, they would have to march through the eastern end of Abath. With no regular east-west roads, the Castol would be forced to construct their own as they marched westward, cutting their way through thick, untamed forest. Such a move would prove a difficult challenge, but, in my mind, not an insurmountable one."

Stiger nodded and saw what the general was getting at. He snapped his fingers. "Unless they use the Inland Sea. They could land an army anywhere along the coast, bypass Abath, march inland, and potentially cut our communications, much like the Rivan attempted. They might even be able to supply themselves by sea."

Treim and Aetius shared a glance. A hint of a smile tugged at the general's lips as he looked back on Stiger.

"Which is why you are going to Thresh," the general said. "We want you to deliver a letter and a package for us."

"You mean to deny the Castol the Inland Sea," Eli said, cocking his head to the side slightly in an extreme manner a human never would. "And if I am any judge, the package you wish us to deliver will be a pile of gold. You humans seem quite fond of that metal."

"Yes, yes we are," Aetius said with a laugh and then sobered. "The empire intends to buy the Thresh for the coming winter and next year's campaign season. We mean to force the Castol to make their way to the front by foot, giving us time to prepare. The emperor is hoping to avoid the expense of having to build a fleet to take Thresh."

"You're not scouting at the moment, so I guess it's okay. But when you are, there are some foods one must avoid," Eli said. "But then again, we've not begun our training, have we? It is only understandable you would not know."

Stiger said nothing to that and instead pursed his lips. Lepidus had been correct. He was beginning to find the elf maddening.

"Also..." Eli sobered and made a show of looking about Stiger's room. "When entering a room, it is always wise to scan it first, even when you think you are safe. Make certain no one is lying in wait. If you do that, you might just live longer."

"I will remember that," Stiger said, and he knew he would. Eli's latest lesson had been well-delivered. Had an assassin been lurking, Stiger knew he would now be dead. And, he had been the target of assassination attempts before. Still, he had tired of the elf's games. "Why are you here?"

"I think you'd best call Tiro," Eli said. "And maybe Father Griggs. It would save time if I don't have to repeat myself."

"You will have to settle for Tiro. Father Griggs hasn't returned from the temple yet," Stiger said. "I was thinking of sending a party to check on him."

Eli gave a half shrug of his shoulders.

Stiger spared another glance at him, suspecting whatever Eli had to say was bad news. Otherwise, he would not be here, and in town to boot. Stiger stepped out into the hall and made his way to the stairs, looking down.

"Sergeant Tiro," Stiger called down. "Sergeant Tiro."

"Sir," Tiro said, appearing at the bottom of the stairs a few moments later. Father Griggs was with him. "Father Griggs just arrived, sir. He'd like to speak with you."

"Come up," Stiger said. "Both of you."

Tiro started up the stairs, with the paladin right behind him.

"What took you so long?" Stiger asked Griggs. "I was about to send a man to look for you."

"I had a lot to talk about with the local priest," Griggs said. "I'm afraid none of what I learned is good."

"Great," Stiger said and led them both to his room. Stiger grabbed one of the lanterns off its mount along the wall.

"I also stayed for evening service," the paladin explained. "Father Senso gives a good sermon. I found myself quite moved."

"A service?" Stiger gestured for both men to enter his room.

"Eli," Tiro said, clearly surprised as he stepped inside. "How did you get here? How did you know where we were?"

"A bird told me and then carried me over the wall"—the elf made a sweeping gesture with his arm—"and through the window. You know, the captain was kind enough to leave the shutter open for me. Otherwise, it would have made it difficult to get in." Eli had innocence written all over his face. He made a flapping motion with both arms, as if to emphasize his point.

"That must have been some bird," Tiro said wryly. "You need to work on your humor. After all these years it's not improved much." Tiro looked over at Stiger. "Elf humor is a little different than ours."

"I like to think it is—how you say? More refined? Yes, I think that's it. Our humor is more refined than yours," Eli said, then gave a respectful nod to the paladin. "Father Griggs, so nice to see you again."

"Eli," Griggs said, his expression drawn and grave.

Stiger closed the door and set the lantern he'd taken from the hallway down on the table. "Right, we're all here. Let's have it, Eli."

"One hundred fifty men slipped out of the town," Eli said, "about two hours ago. I followed them for a bit. They are headed east, moving on the road toward a small forest." Eli paused. "This is the same road we will be taking in the morning and the only one that leads to Haraste from Larensus."

"What do you think they are up to?" Tiro asked, looking over at Stiger.

Stiger pinched the bridge of his nose. He could feel a headache coming on. Without a doubt, he knew what Hanns intended. Was the prefect really that incredibly stupid?

"Sir?" Tiro asked, when Stiger did not answer.

"They are going to set up an ambush," Stiger said. "The prefect means to ambush us."

"An ambush?" Tiro scowled, as if such a thing was inconceivable. "Surely not."

"He won't risk action in town," Stiger explained. "There are simply too many witnesses. He means to catch us on the road with no one about and wipe us out to a man. That way, we won't be able to report on what we've discovered. He hopes to keep the mess he has created quiet by eliminating us."

"Is he mad?" Tiro was appalled. "Order his men to kill legionaries? I don't believe it, sir. I just don't believe it."

"Believe, Sergeant," Stiger said.

"It would be almost impossible to keep such a thing quiet." Tiro was becoming indignant. "Word would be bound to get out and likely from his own men. By nature, soldiers drink, and when they do, they talk. There is no possible way for him to keep this a secret, especially the murder of a Stiger. Begging your pardon, sir."

"You and I know that," Stiger said, sitting down on the table upon which he'd placed the lantern. "However, the prefect is new to the military. He may not realize that yet. Or, more likely, he just does not care."

"But, sir," Trio continued, "do you really think his men would go through with it?"

"They're foreigners, auxiliaries, and poor ones at that," Stiger said. "They look no better than common thugs. If he'd paid them enough, they'd do it and maybe even try to keep their mouths shut, too."

Father Griggs coughed in a meaningful manner. All eyes shifted to the paladin.

"In the last few hours, I've learned a bit about the prefect, nothing good," the paladin said. "That said, are you certain an ambush is what he intends? They may be out to confiscate food stores from local farmers. The prefect has made a side business by profiting off of other peoples' goods. That does not include the bribes he's taking by acting as the region's magistrate. He is making a fortune."

"I can confirm they go to set up an ambush," Eli said. "I must admit, it caught me by surprise. Curious as to what they intended, I snuck up on them when they took a break from marching. If I hadn't overheard several of the auxiliaries talking about the planned ambush, the money they'd be paid, and speculating on what they would use it for… I would never have guessed they meant you ill. It is why I came."

"I see," Griggs said, suddenly seeming bleak. The paladin's pallor had gone ashen. "Then it is worse than I feared."

"The gods must really hate me." Stiger's headache was growing worse. He felt his rage swelling alongside it. His mission had been a simple one. Now, this…

"Blasphemy is never helpful," Griggs chided. "We must look to the gods for strength in such times."

Stiger took a breath and forced himself to calm down.

"You're right, Father," Stiger said, feeling chastened. "What did you learn speaking with Father Senso?"

"The prefect has arrested his own lieutenant," Griggs said. "Lieutenant Makus is being held in the cellar of the Dancing Goat. The tavern is where Hanns lives and has set his headquarters. It seems Makus did not share the prefect's vision for exploiting the locals. The man refused to be bought off."

"I like him already," Stiger said. He could not place the lieutenant's family, which meant, like Hanns, Makus was equestrian.

"The tipping point came about a week ago when Hanns ordered a farmer and his family to be crucified," the paladin continued. "Makus threatened to write the senate. That was when Hanns had him arrested. The word is, he had his lieutenant beaten first in the hopes he'd come around. He didn't."

"So," Tiro said, "not all of the garrison is bad, perhaps just badly led."

"Honestly," Father Griggs said, "I'm surprised Makus was not killed immediately. Though by now, he may have been. The word Father Senso heard is that he still lives." The paladin sucked in a breath. "It is rumored that the prefect tortures his prisoners. The Dancing Goat's cellar has apparently become a place of nightmare. Father Senso told me a number people have gone down there and not come out."

"That's not good," Tiro said.

"Tiro," Eli said, "you are the instrument of understatement."

Stiger's sergeant shot the elf an unhappy look, but said nothing.

"Even the auxiliaries apparently fear the place," Griggs said. "I shudder to think what is truly going on down there." The paladin paused and looked squarely at Stiger. "Now that I know the prefect intends us ill, we must investigate."

"Somehow, I had a feeling you were going to say that," Stiger said, wondering what was really going on in the cellar.

"We must fix whatever is wrong here," Griggs said, "even if we have to go back to the legion to get more men. It is why I was drawn to go with you. I can feel it."

"You mean this might involve the dark gods?" Stiger felt chilled at such a dreadful thought.

"I don't know," Griggs said. "As I said, we have to investigate and rule that out. It may just be that Hanns is too greedy for his own good and just black of heart. Then again, it might be more. Are you still happy I am with you?"

"Of course, Father," Stiger said, without hesitation. "Even more so, now."

"Eli, what were you doing so close to the town?" Tiro asked. "I thought you'd be out looking for the enemy."

"I was," Eli said. "Bren happened across a farmer along the road, bringing the remains of his harvest into town to sell what he could. The man was quite talkative and told him the garrison was responsible for the destruction of the farms and had thieved most of his harvest. So"—Eli blew out a shallow breath—"I figured I would come back and report." Eli glanced from face to face. "It seems we've all made unpleasant discoveries. I knew this trip to Thresh would be exciting. I think we can all agree…Captain, you draw trouble like a moth to flame."

Stiger rubbed at his eyes, feeling the weight of the world upon his shoulders. He thought furiously for a moment, then looked over at Eli.

"Was there an officer with them?" Stiger asked. "Was the prefect with the men who marched out?"

"No," Eli said. "Now that I think on it, I only saw a sergeant. There were no officers. That does not mean he will not join them come morning."

"I wonder if the sergeant that went with them is Karrax?" Tiro said. "He struck me as a mean one, sir. Kinda like Geta, if you know what I mean."

"I got that feeling, too," Stiger admitted.

"Karrax is the prefect's bully and enforcer," Griggs said. "The auxiliaries fear him. He even had Father Senso beat up, after he spoke against what has been going on. Father Senso is not a young man, but he's got spirit. It is a lucky thing the beating did not kill him."

"Beating a priest," Tiro said. "Who does that?"

Stiger had hoped to move on and let the general handle the mess the prefect had created. Hanns had left him no choice and boxed him into a corner. Stiger chuckled grimly.

"Sir?" Tiro asked.

The prefect had tipped his hand and inadvertently given Stiger an opportunity, an invaluable one at that. He looked between Tiro and Eli. "Correct me if I am wrong, but the majority of the garrison is outside of the town."

"That's true, sir," Tiro said. "Unless they come back tonight, which it does not sound like they will."

"I do not know the garrison's full strength," Eli said, "but I would be surprised if there are more men inside the town's walls than out."

"They won't stop us from leaving," Tiro said. "That's for sure. The prefect wants us on that road traveling east. Sir, we're gonna have to leg it back to the legion. Once they figure out we're going west instead of east, they'll come after us. It will be another chase, but we can outmarch them, sir."

"A chase?" Stiger asked, for that was not what he'd been thinking.

"They're auxiliaries after all, sir," Tiro said, "and from the condition of their equipment, I'd guess they're not much for training or practice marches."

"I don't feel like running," Stiger said plainly, "not at all."

"Sir," Tiro said. "That may be our best option."

"I don't think so." Stiger jerked a thumb toward the common room. "Powel said the cohort numbered only two hundred. That leaves fifty in the town."

"Fifty-one," Griggs said. "The prefect's in town too. He's likely at the Dancing Goat."

"Fifty-one against our twenty-eight," Tiro said. "You mean to take the town, don't you, sir?"

"You've seen the condition of the auxiliaries," Stiger said. "I'd bet on our twenty-eight over their fifty-one any day."

"This is town fighting, sir," Tiro said. "It's not like fighting out in the open. It's difficult, dangerous, and ugly. There will be plenty of places to hide, to lie in wait. And, sir, it's dark out. You know how chaotic night actions can be."

"We will have surprise on our side," Stiger said. "They are expecting us to march right out the town gates come morning. The last thing they will expect is for us to strike."

"The tavern is being watched," Eli said. "I had a look around and identified four lookouts. Two on each end of the street."

Stiger glanced over at the ranger, suddenly glad Eli was with them.

"We will have to take them out," Stiger said, "before we make our move."

"I can do it," Eli said confidently, then added, "silently and with no witnesses."

"Sir," Tiro said. "Are you sure about this? They've not done anything to us yet. There is risk with that, beyond swords."

Tiro was right. There was risk in taking action against Hanns before the man had acted against him. The general, or even quite possibly Hanns's friends in the senate, might hold Stiger to account if they disapproved or if he had judged the situation incorrectly. Stiger glanced over at Eli. He was taking a risk here, and not a small one by any means. With what Eli had overhead, there was simply no doubt in his mind. Hanns meant to kill him and his men. It was enough for Stiger. But he knew it might not be enough for others.

"I am more than certain," Stiger said. "We will take this town and stop what's going on here."

"You are making the correct decision, my son," Griggs said. "Though I doubt the general will find fault, I will speak up on your behalf if he does."

Stiger gave a grateful nod. The paladin's word would carry weight, even in the senate. He turned it over once more in his mind. He was confident he and his men could take the town. They would not only need to seize the Dancing Goat, but also the town gate. Then they would have to deal with any auxiliaries not caught up at the tavern or gate, either kill them if they resisted or round them up. It would likely be difficult and just as dangerous as Tiro had said.

"Do you know where the garrison is quartered?" Stiger asked Griggs.

"No," Griggs said. "I did not think to ask such a question."

Stiger looked over at Tiro, who shook his head in the negative.

"Powel will know," Tiro said. "He'll tell us, sir." Stiger gave a nod.

"We cut off the head of the snake," Griggs said, "and the men he sent out in the field to ambush us will no longer be a threat. They will likely run for their lives once they hear we control the town."

"Serves them right," Tiro said. "They will be branded criminals. They'd better run."

"And if they don't?" Eli said.

"We will deal with that problem when it comes." Stiger came off the table and stood. "One headache at a time."

"We may need reinforcement once the fun begins," Tiro said. "I think we should get Powel to roust the militia. Well, that is after we start, sir. I would not want the prefect to be tipped off we're coming for him should one of the militia prove disloyal."

"Will they fight with us?" Stiger asked, remembering the looks he'd gotten from the locals.

"I think so, sir." Tiro barked out a grim laugh. "They certainly won't fight for the prefect."

"Are you sure you can take out the lookouts?" Stiger asked Eli.

Eli ran a finger along the hilt of one of his long, wicked-looking daggers. "It will not be a problem. In the dark, they won't even see me coming." The elf grinned at him, showing his needle-like teeth. "Trust me."

"Right, then," Stiger said, satisfied. "Let's get the men ready for a fight and speak with Powel. We have a town to take."

Chapter Ten

Setting the bottom of his shield down on the floor, Stiger positioned himself to the right of the door that led out of the Nag and to the street. Tiro was with him, as was Father Griggs. The men crowded around behind, ready, waiting. Stiger reached up a hand and tugged on the straps to his helmet, which he'd already tightened and checked twice now. The straps cut tightly under his chin, just as they were supposed to. Battle was no place for a loose helmet.

The men were grim-faced, tense. There was no talking. Gone was the day's weariness from the march, the exhaustion. All eyes were expectantly upon him. The tension was so thick Stiger thought he could almost cut it if he drew his sword.

Eli was out there, somewhere in the darkness, silencing the enemy's lookouts upon the tavern. The auxiliaries of Hanns's cohort had become his enemy just as surely as if they were the Rivan. The thought that imperial soldiers could sink so low rankled him greatly and fed a growing anger toward the prefect. There would be a reckoning between them, for Stiger intended to kill Hanns for what he'd done.

The kitchen door banged open, startling everyone. Stiger reached for his sword as several men around him jumped. Powel emerged wearing an old legionary kit and carrying his shield. There were more than a few curses and chuckles, along with good-natured ribbing amongst his men. Everyone relaxed a fraction. Powel was liked by the men and an ally. There were no hostile looks or words sent his way.

"By the gods, Powel," Tiro exclaimed in an exaggerated manner. "I almost shat myself."

That brought on laughter from the men, which Stiger realized had been his sergeant's intention.

"Sorry 'bout that, Tiro," Powel called with a sheepish expression. He leaned his shield against a table, donned his helmet, and began fastening the straps.

"Do you need to change your tunic?" Stiger asked Tiro. "Before we go, that is."

There was more laughter from the men.

"No, sir," Tiro said, a smile tugging at his lips. "It was a close thing, but I managed to control myself."

Stiger's eyes slid back over to Powel. Though outdated, Powel's mail armor and shield had been lovingly maintained. There was not even a hint of rust. It spoke well of the man that, years after his term of service had ended, he still looked after his kit. Then again, he was captain of the local militia. Appearances had to be kept up and he clearly strove to set the example for his men to follow, which begged the question: How good was the militia?

The tavernkeeper's helmet was from a generation past, more conical in shape and without the long cheek guards that were now standard. His cheek guards were smaller, more rounded. A lion was emblazoned upon the shield Powel carried. That lion was the Fourth's symbol.

Helmet secured, Powel picked his shield up and worked his way through the press of men to Stiger. The men moved aside for him.

Beyond at the kitchen door, Stiger saw Powel's wife and Adera watching from a half-open door. Stiger could easily read the concern in Adeena's eyes, though he only sensed excitement from Adera. She was still too young to grasp the gravity of what was about to happen and how it might impact their lives.

"I wish you'd let me roust my boys now," Powel said. "We could help you do this."

"I can't risk that," Stiger said. "Should one of your men prove disloyal and warn Hanns…"

Powel was silent for a prolonged moment.

"I don't much like it, but I understand, sir." Powel gave an unhappy scowl. "I will get the alarm sounded, quietly and just soon as I can. Per your instruction, my boys will assemble in the square. Once my men are assembled, I will send six files, my best men, to the buildings where the prefect has quartered his men. Those are just behind the Dancing Goat, one street over. The cohort has so few men in the town that I do not think we'll have a problem with them in their quarters, sir. There are likely more than a few drinking in the tavern, which will make our job easier and yours tougher."

"I don't want a massacre, vendettas settled," Stiger said. He knew from his talk with Powel that the Dancing Goat had a back door. He did not need enemy reinforcements making his job more difficult. Though in truth, whatever happened in the tavern would likely be all over by the time Powel's men assembled.

With luck, the men in their quarters would not realize there was a problem until it was too late. Once Powel had them contained, he could deal with them afterwards at his leisure.

"I need time to deal with Hanns," Stiger continued. "Just keep them from leaving their quarters. That is all. Do you understand me?"

"And if they engage us, sir?" Powel asked, looking troubled. "What do you want us to do then?"

"You fight," Stiger said plainly. "I would prefer you keep the prefect's men inside their buildings and out of the fight. After this is over, I will need to justify my actions to General Treim. I do not want to have to explain how your militia butchered men in their quarters. The general may excuse my actions. He certainly will not excuse yours and neither will I."

"I understand, sir," Powel said. "My boys are angry. So are the people of this town. But I will see they stay their hand. We will give you the time you need. You have my word on that."

Stiger gave a nod, satisfied.

"All that said," Powel said, "if you fail, Captain, my people will see it finished. On that I promise."

Stiger gave another nod. He knew that life for these people had become near intolerable. "I would expect nothing less."

"Good that we understand each other," Powel said.

Stiger turned his gaze to Tiro, who was looking back on him. The old sergeant's face was drawn, the humor from a few moments ago gone. His jaw flexed repeatedly, as if he were chewing on something. Only someone who knew the sergeant well would see the signs. Stiger understood the gut-clenching sensation only too well. It was the terrible dread that came before battle.

Stiger's gaze shifted back to the door. Eli had left the tavern well over half an hour ago. The wait, which seemed to go on and on, was frustrating, even maddening. The elf seemed to be taking his sweet old time. Stiger knew that wasn't exactly fair. Eli was to eliminate four men and do it stealthily, without setting off the alarm, a difficult task to be certain. That surely took time, especially if he was to do it right. However, Stiger could not help but feel impatient. He wanted to get moving.

He desperately hoped he had not misplaced his faith in Eli. For if the elf screwed up or was discovered, the game would be up. The goal of surprising and overcoming what was left of the garrison would become more challenging, perhaps even impossible. He had bet his own life and those of his men on Eli.

Stiger suppressed a sigh and focused on remaining calm, something he most certainly did not feel. His thoughts were in a turmoil. His calm demeanor was a façade for his men. He had to appear like he was in control, otherwise they would lose confidence in his leadership and that would prove fatal. Internally, the questions gnawed at him.

Had he made the correct decision? How many of his men would become injured, die? Would he be killed? The waiting was always the worst part, for it gave time for the questions and self-doubt to nag and run through his mind.

On the other side of the door, Stiger could hear the armor of Legionary Kollus chinking as he paced. Kollus, still on sentry duty, had been informed of what was coming. He had been told to remain in position and act as if nothing was wrong. But clearly the waiting had gotten to him too. Standing in the near-darkness of the street, Stiger could only imagine how hard that was for the legionary.

Thinking on what was to come, Stiger took a breath. It was time to look after his soul. He closed his eyes and bowed his head.

"The captain is right." Father Griggs broke the silence, addressing the assembled men. "A prayer and blessing is in order."

Stiger glanced up at the paladin. "Go ahead, Father, a blessing is most welcome."

"Thank you, my son." The paladin spoke in a calm, yet confident tone that Stiger found steadying of heart. "Should you wish to receive the High Father's blessing, kindly bow your heads."

The men dutifully bowed their heads, as did Stiger. The paladin waited a moment more. There was some shifting of feet and the scrape of the bottom of a shield on the wooden floor. Nothing made men more religious than an imminent fight.

"Great Lord and Father, I ask your blessing over these fine men. Strengthen their arms and hearts. Lift up their spirits. Guide their steps and actions this night. Lead them in their duty to you and to the empire. Hold these men close and fill them with your spirit. Shield them from harm and, should a man fall, take his soul into your everlasting and loving embrace." The paladin paused. "Though we do not have a sacrifice, we offer our thanks to you, oh Great Lord, for your love and our lives." The paladin paused for two heartbeats. "We give thanks."

"We give thanks," the men intoned in unison. They shifted about as their heads came back up.

Stiger brought his head up, looking over his men. All eyes swung back to him.

"You know what you need to do," Stiger said to them. "Those going with Tiro will secure the gate, then clear the walls. The rest coming with Father Griggs and myself must take the Dancing Goat. The prefect is our objective. I want to be clear. If any of the auxiliaries offer to surrender, you are to take them prisoner. If they fight, kill them stone dead." Stiger paused. He did not want his men taking any unneeded risks. With the losses the company had suffered this past summer, he could not afford to lose any more veterans. These men and those who remained back at the legion's encampment were the beating heart of his company. "When in doubt, kill. It is that simple and I won't hold it against you. Got that?"

"Yes, sir," the men chorused.

"Good," Stiger said, though he'd already gone over this several times. He'd learned that to get results in the military, it was best to be repetitive. "Once we have the prefect, we'll worry about any stray auxiliaries out in town. The militia, once deployed, should keep most of them corralled in their quarters. For those men going to the gate and wall, don't get separated in the darkness. Stay with your assigned buddy. Got that?"

"Yes, sir," the men chorused again.

"Tiro." Stiger lowered his voice slightly. "Any questions?"

"No, sir," Tiro said.

Stiger knew his sergeant was far from happy at leaving him.

"I will take my men and secure the gate," Tiro said, glancing over at those assigned to him. "We won't go for the rest of the walls until you have Hanns and we're reinforced, either by you or the militia. We will defend the gate and make damn sure it is locked and barred should the bulk of the auxiliary cohort return."

"Good," Stiger said. He wanted to add for the sergeant to take care of himself, but he kept that to himself. It would not do for the men to see him direct such familiarity toward Tiro, though they all knew how much he valued the sergeant. Stiger wasn't sure what he'd do if he ever lost Tiro. The man had proven himself invaluable and a good friend.

For his part, Tiro seemed to understand Stiger's thoughts, for he gave a curt nod.

"We will all do our duty," Tiro said. "Won't we, boys?"

There was a growl of general agreement.

"You are the best," Stiger said. "The best of the best. You proved that this summer. These auxiliaries can't hold a candle to you. Remember your training, trust in your comrades, and you will come through just fine."

Stiger was about to say more, but the door opened. Eli stood framed in the doorway, the light from the common room playing over him. One of his daggers was held loosely in his right hand. Blood dripped from the exposed blade and onto the threshold. There was a hard look upon the elf's perpetually youthful face. He eyes sought out Stiger.

"It is done. The lookouts have been taken care of," Eli said to Stiger as he pulled out a hand towel from a small pack at his side. He began cleaning the blade free of the blood. "It took me a little longer than expected, for I discovered a fifth lookout had been posted in a building overlooking the north end of the street. He needed to be dealt with before I could silence the others." The elf paused. "They never saw me coming."

"Right, good work." Stiger felt immense relief wash over him. He looked back on his men, who had begun picking up their shields. It was time. "Sergeant Tiro?"

"Sir?" Tiro asked.

"Take the gate," Stiger ordered.

"Yes, sir," Tiro said. "My boys with me."

Eli moved aside as the sergeant led his men from the building and out into the darkness.

The elf sheathed his dagger and stepped just inside the door. He retrieved his bow and a half-dozen arrows that he'd leaned against the wall by the door. Eli stepped back into the night.

"Powel," Stiger said. "Go roust your militia. Keep it quiet."

"Yes, sir," Powel said. "I will. Good luck, sir."

Stiger caught the tavernkeeper's arm as he moved toward the door.

"Sir?"

"No butchery." He released Powel's arm. "Keep the townspeople under control, too."

Powel gave a somber nod and left.

Stiger turned back on those remaining with him.

"We hit hard and fast," Stiger said. "Any questions?"

There were none.

"Let's go." Stiger led his men out and onto the street. The night was only lit by a handful of torches, lanterns, or windows from which dim, yellowed light spilled outward. He looked first down the street and then up it in the direction of the town square. It would take some time for his eyes to fully adjust to the darkness.

Tiro and his men were disappearing around a corner, moving onto a side street that led in the direction toward the gate. Beyond that, there was no sense of alarm being sounded. The town was quiet, the air cold. Breath steamed. Thunder from an approaching storm rumbled like a distant cavalry charge and somewhere a dog began barking in reply.

"If you don't mind, I will lead the way," Eli said. "In the darkness, my eyes are better than human eyes."

"You know the way?" Stiger was surprised by that, as Eli had just entered the town a short while before.

"Tiro told me how to get to the Dancing Goat," Eli said with an innocent expression. "Before I dealt with the lookouts, I went and found a good route that runs along several side streets. We should not be seen as we approach the square. At least, I hope so. I did not have much time to do a proper job."

"Really?" Stiger asked, exasperated. "What if they'd caught you or you'd been spotted?"

The elf grinned at him, showing his teeth. "They didn't and that's all that matters."

Stiger let out a breath of pure frustration. He held out his free hand, palm up in the direction of the town square. "Be my guest."

"You want me to stay with you?" Eli asked, the smile replaced by confusion. "As your guest? I would be honored, but now really does not seem the time for such a conversation."

"I meant," Stiger said, feeling the exasperation mount to new levels, "lead the way."

Eli grinned at him again, then turned in the direction of the Dancing Goat and started up the street at a fast walk. Stiger fell in at his side. Eli held his bow in his right hand, along with the arrows. His left was free. Behind them, the men and Father Griggs followed as they made their way up the street.

Two dark shapes appeared from the shadows, slumped against the side of the road. Blood slicked the stones and glistened slightly from the nearest torch ten yards away. The lifeless sentries had been dragged around the corner and to the side, their blood running down the drainage channels like water. Stiger found he had to be careful to avoid it, lest he slip and turn an ankle on the slick stone.

Leaving the bodies behind, they moved quickly through the narrowed streets, almost jogging as they worked their way toward the center of town. Breath came fast with the pace. Hobnailed sandals slapped loudly on paving stones, interspersed with the chink of armor and the occasional clunk of shields banging together. It seemed deafeningly loud in the narrow confines of the street. Stiger felt himself cringing at the noise he and his men made, but in truth knew it would not carry as far as his imagination made it seem.

One of the many doors along the street abruptly opened ahead. The buildings, mostly homes, were built right up against one another in this part of town with no space between. A man wearing a red tunic and carrying a wine jar stepped out into the street. Framed by the light from within, he spotted them coming his way, froze for a heartbeat, then quickly retreated back inside. He slammed the door behind him. From inside, a heavy locking bolt was thrown. Then they were past.

Stiger and his men followed the elf through the winding maze of side streets as he led them toward the square. Eli made a final turn onto a side street from which there was very little light. Ahead, Stiger could see the square. As they neared the end of the street, Eli held up a hand. The motion was clear and they came to a shuffling halt around ten yards from the square.

Eli took an arrow and nocked it, though he held the bow loosely in his right hand, along with the rest of his arrows tight to the shaft. Stiger motioned his men against the wall so they'd not be seen. Eli crept forward the last few feet to the corner. Stiger followed, with Griggs on his heels and the men in a single file right behind the paladin. Eli peeked around the corner rapidly and pulled his head back out of view.

"Four sentries," Eli whispered to Stiger. "All are before the tavern door. There is no one else in the square."

Stiger took a quick look. There were four men, just as Eli had said. They were standing under a lantern that Stiger knew would blind them to the wider darkness. The only other lights in the square came from second-story windows. And of those, such light was very dim and would not be useful. Stiger glanced up at the sky. The moon was hidden behind a thick layer of overcast. He could not have asked for better conditions from which to launch his attack on the town.

The sentries stood talking amongst themselves and were anything but watchful, a serious breach in discipline. He thought they appeared bored. Stiger took another look and studied the distance. It was over forty yards to the tavern entrance, a long way.

"We're gonna have to rush them," Stiger said, not relishing the idea. The four were bound to sound the alarm the moment he and his legionaries stormed into the square. There was no telling how many more waited inside the tavern. Once the alarm was raised, those inside would begin readying themselves. He would have liked to catch them all completely by surprise, but that was not meant to be. This was the best they could hope for. There was simply no helping it. "Yep, we're gonna have to rush them."

"I can deal with the sentries," Eli said softly and hefted his bow.

"All four?" Stiger had doubts. "With your bow?"

Thunder rumbled again, a low growling sound off in the distance.

Eli gave a sort of half-shrug. "It's a challenge to be sure. But without trying...we will never know, will we?"

Before Stiger could reply or stop him, Eli stepped around the corner, knelt, and brought the bow up. The arrow released into the darkness and near-silence of the night with a twang and a departing hiss. Before Stiger could blink, Eli had nocked and released a second arrow. Then a third flashed outward.

Stiger looked toward the Dancing Goat. Under the light of the lantern, he saw Eli's third shot take a man squarely in the neck. He staggered from the impact, as a drunk might. Like a tree felled by an axe, a second man was in the act of falling backward. An arrow had punched through his forehead. None of the auxiliaries were wearing their helmets. Yet another was down, thrashing and kicking violently on the ground.

The last man, uninjured, stared at his stricken mates for a shocked heartbeat, then turned for the door. Eli released his fourth arrow, which smacked into the back of his skull. The impact made a cracking sound, like a hammer on a nail, that could be heard clear across the square. It sent a shiver down Stiger's spine. The force of the arrow strike threw the man forward, onto the paving, where he landed with a clatter of armor on stone.

Stiger blinked and looked over at the elf, shocked by the ranger's skill. It had happened so fast, had he not seen it with his own eyes he would never have credited it possible.

"Great gods," Father Griggs exclaimed softly. "I knew rangers were good, but that was beyond good, Eli."

"It was," Eli said, with no hint of pride, as he stood. He was simply stating a fact. The elf leaned his bow against the wall of the building at the corner and set the rest of his arrows on the ground. He drew his sword as he turned to Stiger. "Shall we go see the prefect? I believe you wish to speak with him."

Stiger remembered himself. "I do. Hanns and I have unfinished business." He half turned to his men, drawing his blade. "Swords."

The men drew their swords and he motioned them forward. He led them charging across the square. Eli and Father Griggs were just behind him.

Fifteen feet from the tavern's entrance, the door swung open. An auxiliary, wearing only his tunic and carrying a sword belted at his hip, peered out. He held a mug in one hand. His eyes widened as he took in the men felled by Eli. Then he saw Stiger and his men rushing forward. The auxiliary threw the mug away, almost tossing it at the charging legionaries, the liquid spilling outward and onto the paving. He cried out a warning and started to close the door with both hands. In the lead, Stiger lunged and using his shield as a battering ram, he slammed it forward. The shield met the half-closed door with a solid *clunk* and forced it back fully open.

Knocked off balance, the auxiliary lurched backward. Stiger moved into the tavern. He punched out with his shield at the man. It connected, pushing him back a couple more steps. The man grunted from surprise and the pain of the blow. He retreated several more steps. Stiger had a glimpse of men clustered around tables. Then shouting rang out as Stiger's men pounded into the tavern after him.

Stiger ignored it all, for the auxiliary he faced had managed to draw his sword and came forward to attack. The auxiliary swung his sword in a clumsy, ill-prepared slashing arc. Stiger blocked and the blade clunked against the shield. He felt the impact of the blade communicated to his arm, behind the shield. The auxiliary aimed a second awkward strike, this one for his head. Stiger raised the shield and neatly blocked the blow. Stiger's arm and hand holding the shield stung from the second strike.

Ignoring the pain, he took a quick step forward and used his shield to knock his opponent's sword aside, then lunged forward, punching out with his blade. The sword point slid into the auxiliary's stomach with force. The man gagged as Stiger's blade went in deep. Their gazes met as time seemed to stop. His opponent's eyes were a pale, almost baby blue. They were wide with pain and shock. It was an intimate moment, only broken as warm blood gushed from the ruptured belly over Stiger's sword hand. He gave the sword a savage twist and yanked it back.

Crying out in agony, the man sank to his knees, a hand held over his ruined stomach, from which torn and bloodied entrails had spilled outward onto the dirty wood floor of the tavern. Stiger knew the wound was a mortal one. Stomach wounds generally were fatal. They were one of the most feared injuries, for those wounded in such a manner tended to linger, sometimes for weeks, in terrible pain before death finally claimed them.

The auxiliary still held his sword and Stiger knew he could yet pose a threat. He kicked him hard to the chest, throwing the man back to the floor. The sword flew free and clattered away, out of immediate reach.

Stiger turned, for the ringing sound of sword on sword caught his attention. His head snapped around, surveying the tavern's common room. The sight that greeted him was one of chaos. There were at least twenty auxiliaries. They had been clustered around four large tables, clearly drinking the night away. None wore armor, but all were armed. Stools and benches had been kicked back. He did not see any civilians.

Stiger's men had moved farther into the room. The legionaries were outnumbered, but they were armored and carried shields, which more than made up their lack of numbers. They were also highly trained killers, and a glance told Stiger the auxiliaries did not stand a chance. Several auxiliaries were already down. Some of the enemy attacked with a ferocity that Stiger found quite surprising, while others, startled or drunk, simply backed away, not quite sure what to do. One of the auxiliaries threw a stool across a table at the legionaries, which was blocked by a shield. Only one man had the presence of mind to run, and that was up the back stairs to the second floor. Where he was going, Stiger had no idea. Perhaps he intended to jump from a window and flee into the night or hide?

Something flashed by Stiger's face, passing so close he felt the wind of its passage against his nose. It was followed almost immediately by a meaty *thwack* to his right. Stiger blinked and looked over. An armed and armored auxiliary, just three feet from him, had opened a door that led to a hallway. So focused was his gaze on the auxiliaries in the common room, Stiger had not even noticed the door. In one hand the man held a raised sword and in the other the hilt of a dagger that had buried itself up to its guard in his neck. He spat up a bloody froth and collapsed back into the room, the door closing on his legs, which kicked and shook violently as he choked to death on his own blood.

Stiger glanced over to the left and saw Eli a few paces away. The elf's dagger had saved him. Eli shot him a wink, then advanced to meet an auxiliary who had some fight in him. The noise inside the tavern was loud, cacophonous. Men cursed, screamed at one another, howled in rage, begged for mercy. Sword clanged against sword or clunked on legionary shields. In the confined space of the common room, it beat on the senses and assailed the ears.

"I am gonna gut you," a massive and powerfully built man with a bushy brown beard and gray service tunic yelled at Stiger and then charged. "Bastard."

Stiger just had enough time to bring his shield up and attempt to brace himself as the man crashed into him. He staggered back a step, the shield forced slightly aside. Stiger jabbed out with his sword. He felt the tip poke into the man's thigh. It only seemed to anger him and he roared with the pain. Then he struck at Stiger again with his sword. Stiger managed to get his shield up, and just barely. The blow on the shield was powerful and left Stiger's arm tingling. The auxiliary aimed a punch at Stiger's head, which he dodged by crouching. The man's large fist sailed harmlessly over his head.

Grunting, Stiger shoved back as hard as he could, pushing the large man back a step. His opponent recovered quickly and, lightning fast, the man's sword banged against the top of his shield. The blow was powerfully delivered and sent a large splinter of shield flying through the air. Grunting and using his shield, Stiger forced his opponent's sword to the side and away. He drew back to jab but the auxiliary was quicker and lunged, seizing Stiger's wrist in a clamp-like hold.

"No you don't," the man spat. "Think to poke me again, did ya, boy? I'll teach you, laddie."

Stiger was unable to free himself. He glanced down and saw the auxiliary wore sandals. He remembered Tiro's instruction on fighting dirty. There was no fairness in war. All that mattered was winning. He stamped down on the man's foot. The auxiliary gave a bellow of pain as Stiger's hobnailed boot crunched downward. The grip on his sword hand slackened a tad. Stiger tore his hand free, stepped closer, and stabbed with all his might, taking the man just under the chest and driving the blade upward behind the ribcage. He felt fresh, hot blood soak his hand and arm as the blade went in.

His opponent expelled a breath, sagged backward, then collapsed to the ground and lay there twitching his last in an expanding pool of blood that gushed outward and onto the floor in steady beats.

Stiger turned to search for another opponent and found things had gone nearly quiet. There were moans and cries of agony from the wounded, but no more sounds of fighting. Breathing heavily, he looked around the tavern and saw that the fight had gone out of the remaining auxiliaries.

Ten men were down on the ground, either unmoving or writhing in pain. One man with a bad stomach wound kept screaming, a harsh, piercing sound that grated at the ears until a legionary kicked him in the head, then silenced him with a sword thrust to the neck. Another auxiliary, bleeding out from a leg wound, wept and whimpered like a baby. He called softly and intermittently for his mother. Stiger saw that one of his men, Kello, was injured, cradling an arm that had been ripped open. The sight of his wounded man got him wondering how the fight for the gate was going.

Stiger forced the thought from his mind. He had work to do and needed to focus on the here and now. Whatever was happening at the gate, he'd worry about later. Tiro likely had everything well in hand.

Stiger returned his attention to the auxiliaries. The uninjured had dropped their weapons and backed away from the bloodied legionaries, moving toward the far wall. They were holding their hands up.

"We surrender, sir," one of the auxiliaries said loudly. "For the gods' sake, we surrender. Don't kill us."

Stiger recognized the man as the corporal he had encountered earlier in the day. Stiger scanned the auxiliaries and did not see Hanns amongst the living or dead.

"If you don't resist," Stiger said, "you will be spared."

"Thank you, sir," the corporal said, his shoulders slumping slightly.

"You two." Stiger pointed at legionaries Vexenus and Makaenen. "Gather up those weapons. Max, go find the other exit, lock and block it. We don't need any uninvited guests. Kenso and Faernun, guard the prisoners." Stiger paused. "The rest of you, search the tavern. Find anyone that's hiding. Get to it."

The men began moving toward the doors and stairs.

"We have to find Hanns," Griggs said, coming over to Stiger. The paladin sheathed his large sword, which was bloodied up to its hilt.

"That's what I intend to do," Stiger said, hoping the prefect had not made an escape. "Corporal," Stiger said and looked over at the prisoner, "where is your prefect?"

The man paled. He swallowed, hesitating to answer as if he were afraid. The other auxiliaries shifted about uneasily.

"Where is Prefect Hanns?" Stiger asked, advancing on the man. Stiger's sword was still out, and the corporal's eyes flicked to the bloodied weapon and then back to Stiger's face.

"In the cellar, sir." The corporal's voice trembled slightly.

"Show me," Stiger ordered.

The man pointed toward the kitchen door, where three of Stiger's men had just disappeared. There were several shouts from within, then the door banged open again. Five civilians, four middle-aged women and one older man in his sixties with a badly stained apron, spilled out, followed by Legionary Antonius. One of the women stopped and shrieked when she saw the bodies and blood-spattered common room.

"Shut your mouth," Antonius shouted and pushed her forward toward the other prisoners. "Over there."

Stiger ignored them, instead keeping his attention on the corporal. The man had not moved. Stiger could read the fear in his eyes, and it wasn't from him and his men. Something else had the man scared nearly stiff.

"Show me," Stiger repeated to the corporal. "I will not ask again."

"Yes, sir," the corporal said nervously and, keeping his hands held up in the air before him, led the way into the kitchen. Stiger followed, with Griggs and Eli on his heels.

The kitchen was good-sized and hot. An oven and cooking fireplace were along the left wall. A small fire crackled in the fireplace, over which hung several iron pots from chains and hooks. Woodsmoke and baking bread was strong on the air, as was the stench of old ale. A large wooden table dominated the center of the kitchen. Part of the table was covered over in flour, with dough halfway through the process of being kneaded. On the right side of the kitchen were several rows of rough-cut shelving. Pots, pans, plates, jars, and cooking implements lay scattered haphazardly over the shelves and table.

The floor was littered with scraps of discarded food, some of which were moldy. It looked like it had been months since anyone had cleaned, or even swept for that matter. Stiger felt sour just looking at the mess and wondered how many people had been poisoned due to the cooks' lack of cleanliness.

Two legionaries, Kollus and Lucius, emerged from what appeared to be a storeroom.

"No one else here, sir," Kollus said. "No doors either."

"Where is the cellar?" Stiger asked the corporal.

"Under the rug at the far end of the room," the corporal said in a resigned tone. "There is a trapdoor under the rug."

"Check under the rug," Stiger ordered and pointed.

Kollus and Lucius stepped over to the rug. He heard an exclamation as Lucius pulled the rug aside. They had discovered a large wooden trapdoor. Kollus pulled at the metal ring and, with a grunt, hauled back the trapdoor until it stood open.

"He's down there, sir," the corporal said. He looked hesitant to go closer. "In the cellar. I don't ever want to go down there again." The corporal lowered his hands and turned to face Stiger. "I'd not recommend going. You can kill me if you want, sir, but I'm not going. Death is better."

Stiger spared the corporal a long look, feeling suddenly uncomfortable with what he knew he needed to do. "Return to the common room."

"Yes, sir," the corporal said with evident relief and beat a hasty retreat, almost running for the door.

Stiger walked over to the trapdoor, which now stood open. Father Griggs and Eli came with him. A line of stone stairs disappeared into darkness. A dim light could just be seen at the bottom. An unpleasant smell wafted upward, as did a chill coolness. It was as if death were reaching forth its beckoning hand from an ancient crypt. Stiger wrinkled his nose. He recognized the stench of rotting flesh, and in the few moments the trapdoor had been opened, it overpowered the kitchen's other smells. Stiger shivered. He wondered what horrors lay in wait.

"I sense wrongness," Griggs said, quietly. "Terrible wrongness."

"I think we can all agree that is an understatement," Eli said.

"I really don't want to go down there, sir," Legionary Kollus said.

"Neither do I," Stiger said with a glance thrown to Kollus, "but we're going."

Chapter Eleven

"Kollus," Stiger said, looking over at the legionary, "you're coming with us."

"Are you sure you don't want to take Lucius, sir?" Kollus asked with a glance thrown to the other legionary.

"That's all right, sir," Lucius said. "Kollus can have all the fun. I don't mind you taking him with you."

"Lucius." Stiger glanced over to the legionary. He knew both men were friends, inseparable as brothers. Normally he'd have been mildly amused but now was not the time. "Find another man, preferably two. Anyone comes up but us, you kill them. You don't ask questions, you kill them. Understand me?"

"Yes, sir." Lucius made for the door, shooting Kollus an amused smirk as he left the kitchen.

"I don't much like the underground." A haunted look crept into Eli's eyes. "Not much."

Stiger could well understand the elf's reservations as he looked back down the stairs. They were dark and, he thought, foreboding. The steps were laid stone rather than poured concrete, and a slight depression in the middle showed years of wear by many feet. The dim light Stiger had noticed at the bottom showed a dusty tiled floor. He took a deep breath through his nose and almost instantly regretted it. The smell coming up from the cellar was plain awful.

"Well," Stiger said, "there is no point in delaying."

Hefting his shield and keeping his sword at the ready, Stiger started slowly, carefully down the stairs. He strained his ears, listening for any hint of movement, anyone lying in wait. He heard nothing, other than his own footsteps and those following him down.

On the last step, Stiger hesitated. A tin-plated lantern hung from a hook along the back wall. Its tiny flame burned almost sullenly. The cellar was surprisingly small for the size of the tavern, ten feet by ten, nowhere near the footprint of the building itself. Stiger would have expected something a little larger.

Like the steps, the walls were stone. Some of the floor tiles had shifted with age as the ground settled and were no longer perfectly aligned or, for that matter, even flat. The space was filled with casks, barrels, and sacks stacked haphazardly about. It appeared as if whoever had carried it all down had just dumped it wherever they felt like, then left. Old stools and benches were stacked upon one another. Stiger even saw a bed frame. Everything was covered over in a layer of dust, which did not seem quite right, for it was almost as if the cellar was no longer used.

Stiger took the last step, peered around, and didn't see anyone. Griggs came next, then Eli, who was followed closely by Kollus. They fanned out around him, studying the small cellar, which smelled of mold, decay, and worse.

"There's no one here," Kollus said with more than a little relief.

Stiger felt himself frown. The cellar was clearly empty. He could not imagine Hanns hiding here. The cellar was so small a child might be able to hide amongst the junk, but certainly not an adult. Stiger sheathed his sword, went to the lantern, and lifted it off the hook. He moved about the small cellar and shined it around, peering behind barrels and stacks of things, looking for something that would explain why they had found the cellar empty.

"Is there another cellar?" Eli wondered aloud.

"I rather doubt it," Stiger said. "That corporal was pretty sure Hanns was down here."

Stiger had the feeling he was missing something. He lowered the lantern, shedding its meager light upon the floor, and saw a footprint in the dust at his feet. He bent down, examining it. Whoever had made the print had been heading in the direction of the stairs and clearly stepped in something dark. Stiger put a hand down and touched the print, feeling the crust of whatever had been left behind. Eli squatted down next to him.

"Interesting find," Eli said. "I believe that's blood."

Stiger moved the lamp in the direction the footprint had come from and found a number of similar tracks leading to the opposite wall. In fact, now that he looked closely, there was a veritable path through the dust that seemed to see regular traffic. To either side of the path, the only footprints were theirs. The tracks led from the stairs straight to the wall.

He exchanged a look with Eli. The elf appeared just as mystified. Stiger and Eli moved over to the wall. Holding the lantern high, Stiger studied the stone. He could see no seams that would indicate a hidden door. There was just plain, unbroken stone. Stiger's gut told him something was not quite right. There was something wrong here, he was sure of it. He reached out a hand toward the wall and, not quite sure why, hesitated.

"Do not touch the wall," Griggs warned.

Stiger snatched his hand back as the paladin stepped up next to him. Griggs sheathed his sword.

"Sometimes," the paladin said, "it takes a light to see in the darkness."

Stiger wondered what the paladin meant by that, especially since they had a lantern. Griggs closed his eyes. The paladin reached out and, with the flat of his palm, touched the stone of the wall. There was a brilliant flash of white light, which startled Stiger. Momentarily blinded, he stumbled back a step, blinking furiously.

His vision cleared and he found himself looking at a hole about waist-high that had been cut through the stone of the wall. It was large enough for a person to climb into, and peering through, Stiger saw it opened into a tunnel. Supported by thick timber beams, the tunnel was big enough to stand upright and walk through without hunching over. It looked about twenty feet long.

"How?" Stiger asked the paladin, amazed. He realized that somehow the hole and tunnel had been concealed from his view. "How did you do that? Magic?"

"Faith, my son," Griggs replied. "Faith and a little help from the High Father."

"Priestly magic," Eli said. "An illusion was cast over the entrance hole. And, if I'm not mistaken, it had the power to injure, if not outright kill."

Stiger glanced to the hole and then back to the paladin. "It should be safe to proceed." Griggs gestured toward the tunnel. "Well, as safe as can be expected. I can't speak for the tunnel's integrity."

Stiger held the lantern up to shine the light through the hole. The tunnel appeared to open up into another space at the end. He could see the glow of light ahead, but it was faint. Stiger glanced over at the paladin in question, who gave an encouraging nod. Stiger pulled himself up through the hole and into the tunnel.

"Careful, my son," Griggs whispered as the paladin climbed in after him. "We don't know what is waiting ahead."

Stiger was about to reply when, ahead, someone screamed. His blood ran cold. It was terrible and agonized. The scream echoed off the walls, making it sound as if it had come from dozens of people. It died off and was followed by echoing laughter. Both the scream and the laugh were muffled, as if they had come from a distance. Stiger took another breath of the fetid air, tightened his grip upon his shield, then moved slowly forward so that Eli and Kollus could climb into the tunnel. As he moved, Stiger shined the lantern before him. He could see dried blood mixed into the dirt at his feet.

As he came to the end of the tunnel, Stiger set the lantern down. The tunnel opened up into a natural cave. Marble steps, at least fifty, led downward to the cavern's floor. The steps looked ancient, far older than the town. They seemed out of place in the cavern, for they were the kind one would find leading up into one of the grand temples back in the capital. Instead, these led downward.

Stiger's gaze moved outward from the steps. Much of the cave was hidden by darkness, which gave a sense that the cavern was quite large. His attention was drawn toward the light around twenty yards off. Six large iron candelabras, each with a dozen fat candles, stood around what appeared to be an altar of some kind. The floor of the cave leading from the stairs to the altar had been laid with marble tile. He could see no one about, but they could be hidden just out of view in the darkness.

"This place is for the worship of Avaya," Griggs said in a hushed tone, sounding certain as he came up and stood next to Stiger. He pointed toward the altar. "The spider there confirms it."

"Avaya?" Stiger asked in the same low tone. Behind them, Kollus muttered an oath. "The dark god? How can you tell?"

"Look closely at the altar," Griggs said. "On the floor before it is a painted spider. That is one of the goddess's chosen representations on our world."

Stiger looked at the floor. In the dim light he could make out long lines painted on the ground and stretching out from the altar. It took him a moment to see them as the eight spindly legs of a giant spider. He felt his heartbeat quicken. Stiger disliked spiders. He cleared his throat, for it almost certainly made Hanns a follower of that dark and evil goddess.

"I would not be surprised if, long ago," Griggs said, "a temple to Avaya stood where the tavern is now, for this place is ancient. Now we know why the High Father sent me along with you."

Another muffled scream filled with terrible agony echoed about the cavern. Stiger could not pinpoint from where it originated.

"I think it's coming from over there," Griggs said and pointed to the immediate left, down and along the wall of the cavern. Stiger looked and saw a passageway had been cut into the wall about ten feet from the marble staircase. It appeared to lead down, deeper, and there was light coming from it. "We must be cautious, for there will surely be enemies ahead."

Stiger stared at the passageway for a long moment. This was the last place he wanted to be, and he most certainly did not want to go down the stairs. He shot a quick look behind him at Eli and Kollus. Stiger rubbed his jaw as he turned his gaze back to the altar. He bent down and picked up the lantern.

"We don't belong here," he said to them. "We came to do a job and need to see it through."

"That we do, my son," the paladin said with a grim hardness.

"I'm with you, sir," Kollus said.

"As you said earlier"—Eli shot a smirk his way and gestured down the stairs—"be my guest and lead onward, fearless leader."

Stiger flexed his grip on the shield and started down the steps, taking them slowly, peering into the dark recesses of the cave. He could see no one about. He glanced back at the others. They moved quietly, hushed. Both Eli and Kollus had their swords out. Griggs carried a mace that seemed to pulsate almost lazily with a soft inner light. Stiger came close to missing a step. He had not seen the mace before and wondered where it had come from.

"This, my son, is a holy weapon," Griggs explained, having caught Stiger's look. "It can be called only in times of great need."

Stiger paused on the last step and looked back on the paladin. "This is one of those times?"

Father Griggs gave a shrug. "We had best stay clear of the altar and make right for the passageway."

The scream sounded again, this time lasting for a good long while. Stiger moved around the steps toward the passageway. He stopped at the entrance and looked into another tunnel, like the last, only this one was angled downward at a steep but negotiable grade. A lantern had been hung halfway down the tunnel, which was much longer than the last. He judged the distance to be around fifty yards from entrance to end. There were fresh footprints in the dirt floor and other strange animal-like marks.

"Recognize those tracks?" Stiger asked Eli in a quiet tone.

The elf shook his head.

"Right then," Stiger said, wondering what strange creatures might live in the cave. "Best get to it."

He entered the tunnel and began moving quietly toward the other side. It led to another cavern, this one smaller. Stiger stopped at the end of the tunnel and looked out. A pair of iron candelabras lit much of the cavern. The smell of rotting flesh was overpowering. Body parts and bones littered the floor, as did discarded clothing that had been ripped apart. The walls of the cavern to the left and right had been fixed with iron rings from which hung rusted chains and manacles. Some of the manacles still held the remains of bodies or half-rotten limbs.

Stiger was horrified. Bile rose up in his throat. He had never seen anything like this. He fought to keep from being ill. The sensation mixed with a terrible fear that stole over him, for he was in an evil lair and most certainly did not belong. He wanted nothing more than to turn and go back.

The scream sounded again, this time much closer. It was followed by a wicked laugh. Stiger looked beyond the candelabras and saw three figures at the far end of the cavern. He recognized Hanns, but not the two other men. One of the men was bent over someone who was bound and lay upon the floor. The other stood next to Hanns and watched whatever the first was doing. Hanns gave another laugh.

"Slowly," Hanns chided. "Not too quick there, my friend. Life can be such a fragile thing. I said slower."

Stiger ground his teeth, the fear receding as his anger surged. He had heard stories of the black rites practiced by the followers of the dark gods, but he'd never thought to see such things. Was this some sort of religious ritual or just Hanns's sick idea of entertainment?

Until this moment, such things had seemed like stories mothers told to scare their children into good behavior. As he gazed upon the horror before him and the people responsible for perpetrating it, Stiger understood such evil was only too real. His anger turned to rage. Rage turned to determination. There was no reason for any of this. How could any god condone such acts? His gaze settled upon the prefect, and his anger burned white hot. Hanns was a cancer that needed to be rooted out.

Stiger started forward, only to be arrested by Griggs, who gripped his arm.

"We must be cautious," the paladin whispered.

Hanns turned around at that, either having heard something or sensing the newcomers' presence. The prefect wore only a tunic. He carried no weapon. An amulet in the shape of a spider hung from his neck by a gold chain. The amulet was set with a dark gem that had been shaped into an hourglass. It glittered against the candlelight. Stiger's eyes flicked to the prefect's two companions. Neither wore armor and they weren't armed, either.

"Welcome," Hanns said expansively, holding his arms out wide. It was as if the prefect had been expecting them. He showed no surprise whatsoever. "The great goddess Avaya welcomes you to her temple. We welcome all newcomers seeking to bask in her glory. However, you missed morning devotion. If you wouldn't mind coming back later"—Hanns glanced down at his bound prisoner—"I am a little engaged right now. I have some punishment to finish administering."

"This is no temple," Griggs said. "This is a den of disgrace and we're not leaving."

"I had heard a priest came with the captain." Hanns paused to suck in a breath. "Think what you want, priest. All lies in the eye of thou who beholds. So sayeth the goddess in her scripture. To those of the faith it is the High Father who is an evil, dark, and vile god. In this place, priest, you are the one bringing the darkness with you. I bid you tread with care, for you are in her house and not your own."

Stiger had heard enough. He set the lantern down, drew his sword, and began advancing across the cavern, carefully picking his way through the field of bones and rotting body parts. The smell and sight made him want to vomit. Only his determination kept him going. To his right, Griggs kept pace with him. Eli came up on his left, sword held ready. A quick glance told him Kollus was a couple steps behind.

The person they had been torturing moaned. Stiger saw it was a woman. Her dress lying discarded next to her in a crumpled heap, she lay naked and bound on the cold stone floor. Her body was covered over in bruises. She had numerous cuts along her torso and legs that could have been from knives, but Stiger saw none.

The two men with Hanns were shirtless and their skin was slicked with blood, their gray pants covered in old and fresh dark stains. Stiger couldn't imagine how they could get so much of her blood on them. They even had blood smeared on their faces. It dripped from their chins.

The woman abruptly arched her back. Stiger could only imagine the agony that had been inflicted upon her. She gave a feeble cry that died off into a choking fit, then lay still.

Hanns looked down upon her and gave a dramatic sigh. "A pity. She expired far sooner than I desired. My associates were a little too eager. They liked her blood too much, you see."

Stiger's hands began shaking. It was not from fear, but the terrible rage that roiled beneath the surface, threatening to explode. This was an abomination to everything he'd known. He tightened his grip on his sword.

"You don't need your weapons to offer devotion," Hanns said. "It is a sin to bring weapons into the temple."

"We've come to end this madness," Stiger grated back.

"End it?" Hanns chortled, highly amused. "It's only just begun. This, my dear captain, is but the first act."

"I've come to end you, Hanns."

The prefect laughed deeply. It devolved into a mad sort of cackle that cut off. The prefect's face twitched violently. His eyes lost their focus for a moment, then fixed back upon Stiger. Hanns reached up and fingered the amulet hanging over his chest.

"You think to end me?" Hanns asked. "To stop my glorious work? I don't think so."

"Your work?" Griggs asked as they continued forward toward Hanns and the two men. Their eyes had a flat quality to them, as if on the inside they were not really living but had long since expired. Their chests, slick with blood and gore, reflected the candlelight. They held perfectly still, almost seeming not even to breathe.

Stiger, Griggs, Eli, and Kollus moved around the candelabras, closing the distance.

"My work is so very important," Hanns said, spittle flying, and held out both arms to encompass the room. "I was chosen to uncover this temple, to spread the good word and return the goddess to her glory. There was a time she alone was preeminent and her faith dominant on this world. That is my holy task, my life's quest."

Hanns suddenly gripped the amulet tight, as if he were going to rip it from around his neck. His hand glowed red with light from within, like you might see when holding a hand toward the sun. A wall of purple darts shimmered into existence before Hanns, hovered a moment as they solidified, then shot forth toward Stiger. Father Griggs lunged forward and held up a palm toward the attack. The darts froze in midair. Griggs waved in a negligent manner and the darts faded away to nothingness.

"How?" Hanns demanded in astonishment, stumbling back a step, his eyes upon the paladin. "You are no hapless priest, are you?"

"No," Griggs said. "I am not."

"The goddess will reward me greatly," Hanns said, recovering, "when I bring you low, paladin."

"Where is your priest?" Griggs gestured toward the amulet. "That bauble tells me you are an acolyte, nothing more than a glorified follower, one slightly more elevated than the rest of the pond-feeding scum."

Hanns's eyes narrowed dangerously, then flicked around the cavern. The prefect caressed the spider-shaped amulet with a finger. The light from it had gone. His face twitched violently for a heartbeat, then stilled.

"Your words, priest, bother me little, for what you say is true," Hanns said. "My faith is strong. My goddess has honored me greatly with this gift, this holy talisman, a relic from another age. You cannot withstand her power. No one can." Hanns gave a crazed laugh. "Seek to stop me, will you? Others, my former lieutenant included, tried and failed. Soon you, like Lieutenant Makus, will feed my pets." Hanns cackled madly again. "You will feed my pets. It is a great honor, I assure you."

Stiger's gaze flicked to the two men with Hanns. They seemed suddenly eager. One licked his lips in anticipation, while the other bared his yellowed and rotten teeth. They each took a shambling step forward, but the prefect held up a hand and they stilled to immobility, as if frozen in place.

Hanns flashed a smile devoid of humor. It was cruel, debased, and what Stiger decided was pure evil. The prefect closed his fist around the amulet. His hand once again flashed with a dull red light.

"It is time to feed, my lovelies," Hanns said and looked up toward the ceiling. He cackled again, face twitching madly. "Time to feed."

There was a sudden clicking sound from directly above. Stiger looked up and caught a flash of midnight black shapes dropping down, right on top of them. He reacted instinctively, diving to the right, rolling amongst the limbs and bones. Something landed hard, with a heavy thud, just where he'd been. There was a thump and clatter of armor on stone. Kollus screamed. His scream abruptly cut off.

Stiger rolled over a rotting leg that had long since been severed from its owner. It squished sickly under his armor. He paid it no mind as he came up into a crouched position. He'd lost his shield, but held his sword before him, ready. Out of his peripheral vision, he had a flash of Eli diving away and Father Griggs swinging his mace with both hands. There was a blinding flash of white light, followed by a deep crack. Some sort of a creature gave off an inhuman scream.

Stiger blinked away the spots and froze, horrified to his core, not quite believing his eyes. A black spider the size of a large dog faced him no less than five feet away. Eight unblinking eyes were fixated upon him. Stubby hairs covered its carapace. The creature flexed its razor-sharp mandibles and opened its maw, as if eager to eat. Then the spider began advancing, each leg clicking against the stone as it closed the distance between them. Stiger took several hasty steps backward and almost tripped over a half-rotted body, the skin having swelled and recently burst. He stepped over the remains and continued backing up.

Behind the creature, Eli faced an even larger spider. The elf held his sword out toward the spider's face. The creature seemed to recognize the weapon as a threat and was moving slowly sideways around the elf. Eli turned with the creature, keeping his sword before him. A third spider was over Kollus, who no longer moved. The spider straightened, a large chunk of flesh in its mandibles. Its maw opened and it swallowed the flesh. It turned shockingly fast and sprang at Griggs. The paladin dodged aside and batted the creature away with his free arm. Stiger saw the paladin had already killed a spider. The creature's body was broken in two parts and smoked, the legs twitching feebly.

The spider facing Stiger hissed menacingly. Stiger's eyes snapped back to the creature. Black liquid ran from its mandibles. The liquid dripped onto the cavern's floor. It was the liquid that had caused the hissing, not the spider itself. He knew it could only be venom.

Stiger took a step back to gain more space, thinking on how best to kill the creature. As he did, the spider sprang for him, almost flying through the air as it launched itself forward. He dodged to the left, swinging his sword out in a slashing attack, hoping to catch some of its legs. He missed and his sword connected just over the legs. The creature's carapace, like armor, deflected his blade. His attack did succeed in knocking the spider to the ground, where it landed on its side, almost rolling completely over onto its back.

It scrambled to right itself. Before it could come at him again, Stiger dove for it, reaching the eight-legged creature as it righted itself. Using both hands, he drove his sword down hard on the spider's back, point-first, and threw everything he had into it. There was a moment of resistance, then the spider's carapace cracked and the sword drove deep.

The spider screamed, a high-pitched sound, and staggered under the blow. Half of its legs on the right side stopped working. The other legs scrambled frantically, as if to draw away from its tormentor. Stiger had the deadly thing pinned. Placing a firm hand on the spider's broken carapace, he forced it down to the ground, putting his weight into it. He pulled the sword out. Black fluid sprayed across his face and coated his arms. The creature, despite his efforts, forced itself up to stand and began to turn around, legs scrabbling madly at the floor, mandibles quivering.

Screaming his fury, Stiger stabbed down again into the creature's body and then again. The spider screamed and attempted to snap back at him, but Stiger could feel it weakening. He stabbed again and again. Then, finally the nightmare collapsed to the floor and moved no more. Exhausted, Stiger almost fell over the dead spider.

There was a flash of light, followed by a crunching sound. Remembering there was still a fight on, Stiger looked around. The paladin had dispatched the second spider that had killed Kollus. Stiger looked over at Eli, in case he needed help. As he did, the elf drove his sword into the last remaining spider's face. The creature seemed to shiver, then fell still, its legs curling in upon itself as it died. The elf withdrew his sword and shook the viscous liquid off the blade. Or he tried to. It seemed to cling to the steel.

Stiger then saw Kollus. His legionary's throat had been ripped out. He'd been a good man and had been with the company since Stiger had joined it. Kollus had not deserved to die this way, here in this dungeon of horrors. The sight of his man dead reignited Stiger's rage and drove away the exhaustion. He had unfinished business and turned for Hanns, who had backed away. The prefect looked horrified at what had been done to the spiders.

"My pets," Hanns gasped, then roared, his voice echoing off the cavern walls. "What have you done? My pets. She gave them to me. I raised them, fed them. I loved them."

"You will be joining them shortly. I am going to do to you what we did to them." Stiger advanced on the prefect.

"Kill him," Hanns snapped. The two shirtless men started forward toward Stiger, eager looks in their eyes.

Stiger met them. Careful to avoid the ribs, lest his sword become stuck between bone, he slammed his blade into the belly of one, ripping open the stomach. The man grunted from the blow and doubled over. Stiger pushed him off the sword and threw him aside as the other man lunged forward, grabbing for Stiger's sword arm. Stiger twisted to the side and slammed his fist into his opponent's jaw. The man went down without a sound.

Stiger turned toward the prefect, but stopped when he saw the man he'd stabbed get to his feet, his intestines spilling out onto the floor. It was as if he'd risen from the dead. The terrible sword wound to the stomach did not seem to trouble him in the slightest. Before Stiger could react, Father Griggs hit the man hard with his mace in the side of the head. There was another flash of light and the man crumpled, lying still.

"Now, Prefect," Stiger growled, turning back to Hanns. "You have a lot to answer for."

"My mistress will end you for this," Hanns said, though his words lacked conviction. "You will die screaming, begging for mercy as so many others. On this I swear."

"She may get me," Stiger said, "but I'm gonna get you first."

Lightning fast, Stiger punched out with his sword. The prefect attempted to jump back from the strike, but Stiger had been too quick and Hanns too slow. The tip of the blade tore open his throat. Hanns staggered back a step, blinking. Blood spurted and poured out from the wound. The prefect brought both hands up to his throat, attempting to desperately staunch the flow. He choked and gagged. Then, the light of life seemed to leave his eyes and he fell heavily onto his side, where he lay twitching feebly as the blood began to pool around him.

Stiger took a breath and looked around the cavern of horror. His eyes stopped on the spider he'd killed. Even before this, he'd never much been a fan of the eight-legged creatures, now less so. He gave an involuntary shiver.

With the prefect's death, the rage left in a rush, leaving him thoroughly and completely exhausted. Eli knelt next to the man Stiger had knocked out and neatly slit his throat. He died without ever regaining consciousness, his lifeblood flowing out around him.

Father Griggs looked around. The mace had disappeared. Where it had gone, Stiger had no idea. Their gazes met and Stiger read a terrible sadness in the other's eyes. There was no sense of triumph at having defeated the servants of a dark god.

"Were you bitten?" Griggs asked.

"I don't think so," Stiger said, looking himself over. He knew that in the heat of battle men could become seriously wounded and not notice until it was all over. He was a mess, covered over in blood and gore, but none of it, thankfully, was his. "I'm fine."

The paladin looked over at Eli.

"I am uninjured," Eli said.

"I suppose if you had been bitten"—the paladin poked one of the spiders with his boot—"you'd know. These nasty buggers are called Krata. They generally hunt in packs and at night. You find them high in the mountains and away from civilization. Their bite is venomous. So much so, it would stop your heart in a matter of minutes."

"I see," Stiger said. He had seen horror in battle, but this cavern was more than that. Stiger felt a strong desire to return to the surface. In truth, the desire had never left him, but now intensified. He looked over at Griggs. "Is it over? With Hanns dead, have we ended the evil?"

"Here, yes," the paladin said. "I sense the immediate threat is over. Somewhere out there is a priest of Avaya. He will continue to cause trouble until he is found and dealt with. The priest will be much more dangerous than an acolyte."

"Could it be that merchant, Taliman?" Stiger asked.

"It might be." Griggs let out an unhappy breath. "It might not be. Such dark priests conceal themselves well. It is rare to discover such a person, for they generally do not want to be found and cover their tracks. He will have the brand of the spider, on his right shoulder, as I am sure Hanns does. All followers of Avaya do. It is her mark, her commandment to the faithful."

"The brand of the spider?"

Father Griggs moved over to Hanns. Careful not to touch the amulet, he exposed the man's shoulder. There was a small tattoo of a spider, like the painted one before the altar in the other cavern. "Anyone in service to Avaya will have this mark."

"We will need to search the town," Stiger said, glancing around at the horror that surrounded them. "See if this Taliman is still around. At the very least, he will have some answering to do for his partnership with the prefect. I don't believe the senate will be pleased to learn of their arrangement."

"I would appreciate you checking the prisoners," Griggs said. "If you find a man with such a mark, he is to be bound until I can deal with him or killed if he resists. If he is killed, leave the body for me to check for contamination. Touch nothing."

"Contamination?"

"He means that evil may spread through the direct contact of religious devices, such as that amulet." Eli gestured with his sword toward Hanns's body. There was a serious look of distaste upon his face.

"Quite right, Eli," Griggs said. "Contamination has been known to change people, to alter their minds so they think differently, become more receptive to evil. An amulet like that will be looking for a new master, someone to dominate."

"So," Stiger said, "Hanns may not have always been evil? Is that what you are saying?"

"He may have just been a selfish, greedy person all his life and come to own that amulet, intensifying his desire to amass wealth," Griggs said. "That might have begun his slide from the light. Or he happened across a priest and was corrupted. Then again, he may have always been a servant of evil, hiding in plain sight. I am afraid there is no way to tell for certain, especially now that you've killed him."

There had been no condemnation in the paladin's tone. He was just stating a fact. Griggs stepped nearer to Hanns's body. He placed both hands on his hips and gazed downward. "I will have to deal with that amulet, too, make certain it will never be a threat again. That will take a lot of effort." He looked up at Stiger. "Will you do as I asked, Captain?"

"It will be done," Stiger said. "I will impress upon my men the need to be careful."

"Thank you," Griggs said and returned to his examination of the spider amulet.

Stiger moved over and knelt down next to his fallen legionary. Kollus's eyes were open, fixed at the ceiling, the pupils impossibly wide. He felt a twinge of sadness wash over him. Here was another shade to haunt his nights.

"High Father," Stiger said softly, "welcome this man's soul and keep him close. He was a good soldier."

Stiger reached out and closed Kollus's eyes. He stood and found Eli had come up next to him. The elf placed a hand upon his shoulder. "I am sorry your man died. He gave his life doing his duty and helping to right this wrong."

"I know," Stiger said. "That still does not make his loss any less painful. He was down here on my orders."

"He died because it was his time," Eli said firmly. "As a leader, you make decisions. It's your job. When you make the wrong decisions, people will die. Even when you make the right decisions, people may die. It comes with the job you took."

"You sound like Tiro," Stiger said.

"Tiro is wise for a human," Eli said, his gaze flicking to Kollus's body. "We each have our allotted time. When it's up, it's over. The soul moves on to the next journey. That is all there is to it."

Eli's lips twitched with sudden amusement, his eyes roving over Stiger.

"What?" Stiger asked.

"You need another bath," Eli said.

"Right," Stiger said, feeling his mood lighten just a tad. He shook his head at the elf.

Eli grinned full on, then suddenly sobered, his eyes going beyond Stiger. The elf stepped away. "She lives."

Eli rushed over to the woman. Stiger had forgotten her and had assumed she'd died. He followed after Eli, who knelt by her side. She was clearly young, in the prime of her life. She moaned.

"You're going to be fine," Eli said in a soothing voice and began cutting free the bonds that had tied her hands and feet. "Everything's going to be fine."

Stiger looked upon her, feeling a great sadness tugging upon his soul. Her body had been broken. Her face was turned toward the wall and she was crying softly, shoulders shaking. She had been slashed and beaten. The wounds in her belly were bad. Intestines had been exposed. Dark blood oozed out, as well as other fluids. She'd been cut in such a way that death had been intended to be slow and torturous. It saddened him greatly, yet he knew Hanns would no longer be harming anyone else. She would be his last victim.

Next to her body lay a necklace with a silver eagle as its centerpiece, the symbol of the High Father. The necklace had been ripped off, the chain broken. Stiger took a deep breath. He

He knelt beside the girl. Her breath rattled softly as she cried and moaned. She seemed to become more aware, sensing their presence, for she attempted to move and gave a slight moan. Stiger drew his dagger, prepared to end her suffering.

"No," Eli breathed, gripping his wrist.

"She deserves not to suffer," Stiger said. "No one does. If you can't bring yourself to do it, I will."

"No," Eli insisted. He looked back at the paladin. "Father, can you help her? Heal her?"

Griggs had been absorbed examining the amulet. He had not touched it, but his gaze seemed intense. He looked up, blinked several times, and stepped hastily over. As he did, she turned her head, eyes fluttering open, and looked at Stiger. Through the damaged and beaten face, he recognized those eyes, and with it, his heart plummeted. It was the slave girl, Hela, he had saved earlier in the day.

"Help me," she spoke in a whisper, voice hoarse from screaming. "You promised."

Stiger did not know how to respond. This was his fault, he realized. She had suffered because he'd intervened. She reached up a hand that shook violently. Several of the fingers were broken and bleeding. The bone poked through the skin of her left pinky finger. Despite that, Stiger picked up her necklace and placed it in her palm, then took the hand, gingerly, so as not to cause her any more pain, in his own. Her hand was small and cold as winter ice.

"I'm sorry." Stiger cleared his throat. "I'm so very sorry. This is my fault. Had I not intervened earlier with the prefect's men…"

Eli looked over at Stiger sharply, eyebrows raised.

"High Father," she breathed, not seeming to have heard him. "It hurts so."

She coughed up bloody spittle, her back arching once again in pain.

"Can you help her, Father?" Eli asked again.

"I might be able to help." Griggs reached over, laid a hand upon her forehead, and briefly closed his eyes. The paladin removed his hand, then carefully separated Stiger's hand from hers. Griggs took her hand in both of his, almost cradling it.

"Can you heal her?" Stiger asked, hoping desperately the paladin could.

"I will make no promises," Griggs said, voice grave as he checked her pulse. "Her spirit may be too far gone. I will do what I can. At the very least, I will ease her suffering and help her cross over. Now, you're wasting my time. You must not disturb me. I need time and peace. Make certain I get it."

"Peace?" Stiger said. "How can you get that down here? Surely it would be better to get her out of here first."

"I don't think we can move her," Griggs said. "Trust me in this. The High Father brings me peace, even in this dark place. Now leave me be. Time is of the essence, for I can feel her lifeforce ebbing."

The paladin turned back to Hela and placed a hand upon her forehead. Almost immediately, she relaxed, her eyes closing as if going into a deep sleep. Her breathing became more regular.

Stiger stood and took two steps back, his gaze fixated on Hela. When the paladin had removed her hand from his, the necklace had come free and fallen to the floor. Stiger picked it up. He gazed at it for a long moment, then closed his fist around the eagle. This was his fault, no one else's.

"Leave this place," Eli said, standing as well. "Hanns is finished. It's time for you to take charge of securing the rest of the town." The elf paused, and his tone became gentle. "I will watch over them both."

Stiger hesitated, glancing around. He wondered if any other spiders were lurking about, concealed by the darkness. Were they waiting to attack?

"It's all right," Eli assured him. "Father Griggs would not attempt a healing were he not sure the immediate threat was over." The elf's look suddenly became sardonic. "Though I will admit the thought of sending additional men down here to help me stand watch brings me great comfort."

Stiger said nothing, his gaze sliding back to Hela.

"I have lived a long time," Eli said, following his gaze. "In all my years, I have seen some terrible things. This is amongst the worst. I am pleased I had a hand in ending such evil. Today, we have done a great deed. Hold to that. We have made this world a better place, and one cannot ask more than that."

Stiger gave Eli a wooden nod and sheathed his blood- and gore-encrusted sword. He would worry about cleaning it later. He walked over and picked up his shield.

"I will see you on the surface," Stiger said.

"Count on it," Eli said.

Stiger made his way back to the cellar. He paused a moment at the stairs that led up to the kitchen and sucked in a shuddering breath. It was as Eli had said. They had defeated something truly evil this night, done some real good. So why did he feel like he'd failed?

Stiger opened his fist and looked down on Hela's necklace. The High Father had been with them this day. He tucked the necklace into his armor, feeling incredibly frustrated. In the light that filtered down into the cellar from the kitchen, he took another steadying breath. Stiger made his way up the stairs. There were three legionaries in the kitchen.

"Sir?" Legionary Lucius inhaled, looking in apparent shock as he took in his captain. The other two had similar reactions. "Are you okay?"

"I'm fine," Stiger said, glancing back down the way he'd come. "Prefect Hanns was a servant of Avaya."

"Good gods," Lucius said as Legionary Vexenus made the sign of the High Father.

"The gods were with us this night," Stiger said. "The threat is over. Father Griggs is attempting to heal a badly injured woman who was held captive. You three go down and make sure he is guarded. Be warned, it's ugly down there. Touch nothing, for evil may corrupt your soul if you do."

"Evil?" Vexenus asked in a whisper. The legionary's gaze went to the stairs. "Truly, sir?"

"Also," Stiger said, then hesitated a moment as he considered Lucius. "Bring Kollus's body up. He died bravely. I don't want him left down there."

"Yes, sir." Lucius's throat caught. He glanced away a moment, then turned back. Stiger was not surprised to see tears. There was no shame in mourning a fallen comrade, or friend. Stiger was suddenly reminded of Varus.

"We will look after Father Griggs and Kollus, sir," Vexenus said.

"Good man," Stiger said. "Lucius, go see to your friend."

Lucius gave a miserable nod. The men filed down the stairs into the basement. Stiger paused a moment more, listening to their steps fade away. It never got any easier. He returned to the common room and leaned his shield against the wall just outside of the kitchen door. His legionaries were guarding the prisoners, who had all been made to sit, even the civilians who had been found in the kitchen. All eyes fell upon him.

"Bloody gods," one of the women cried out at his ghastly appearance.

"Quiet, you," a legionary snapped.

No one said anything after that, not even his legionaries. They were clearly wondering what the heck had happened. Stiger did not care. He did not feel like talking about it right now. Later, there would be time.

He saw a small table off to his left. There was a pitcher and two mugs resting upon it. He realized how incredibly thirsty he was. He stepped over, picked up the pitcher, and sniffed at it. It was wine. He poured himself a drink, then drank it completely down in one go. He filled the mug again and drained it. The wine was poor and bitterly sour. Stiger barely tasted it. He was so incredibly thirsty it could have been muddy water and he'd have drunk it.

The door opened and Legionary Jax entered the tavern. He looked around, spotted Stiger, and walked over. The legionary's eyes narrowed as he approached.

"Sergeant Tiro's respects, sir." Jax saluted. "He reports the gate is in our hands, sir. He requests reinforcement to clear the walls."

"Very good," Stiger said. "Tell him Prefect Hanns is dead and the tavern is ours. Soon as I can, I will send reinforcement. It will mostly be militia."

"Yes, sir." Jax saluted, then paused. "Sir, there is something else."

"What is it?" Stiger asked.

"Sergeant Tiro was wounded, sir."

"What?" Stiger set the empty mug back down, exhaustion and thirst forgotten. "Badly?"

"No, sir," Jax said. "It's a minor wound. He'll be hobbled and limping about for a few days. He did not want me worrying you with it, sir. But I thought you ought to know."

"Thank you, I appreciate that," Stiger said, relaxing. "Tell Tiro I will make my way over shortly after the garrison's quarters are secured. Dismissed."

The legionary saluted again, then left the tavern.

Stiger ran his gaze around the common room. Everyone was still watching him. His eyes swept over the prisoners on the other side of the room, then stopped on the auxiliary corporal. Stiger felt his rage flare.

"Bring him to me," Stiger snapped and pointed. "The corporal. I want a word with him."

Two of his men stepped forward, gripped the corporal, hauled him to his feet and dragged him over. They forced him to kneel before Stiger. He read abject fear in the other man's eyes.

"What did I tell you?" Stiger asked him quietly. "What did I tell you earlier today?"

"Please, sir, it wasn't my fault."

Stiger cuffed him hard across the face with the back of his hand. The corporal collapsed to the floor.

"Please."

"What did I tell you?" Stiger roared, leaning over the man. He gripped him by the tunic and hauled him to his feet. The corporal cried out, almost gibbering in fear. Stiger punched him in the stomach and allowed him to collapse. He gagged on the floor, attempting to suck in a breath. It felt so satisfying beating this man, taking his frustration out on him. He deserved what he had coming to him.

"I will not ask you again," Stiger shouted. "What did I tell you?"

"She was not to be harmed," the corporal gasped. "Please, sir. I was only following orders. The prefect found out about it. I could do nothing."

Stiger could plainly read the lie in the man's eyes. It only served to fuel Stiger's rage.

"And the rest?" Stiger demanded. "What else did I tell you?"

"That you'd hold me responsible," the corporal quailed, shaking. His lip was split and bled profusely down onto his tunic. "Don't kill me, sir."

"You weren't afraid to die a short while ago," Stiger snarled at him. He thought of the broken girl below and of the other horrors he'd witnessed in Avaya's temple. He hauled the man up and ripped his tunic on the right shoulder. There was nothing, just pox-marked skin. Infuriated, Stiger punched him again in the gut, knocking him back to the floor. The corporal cried out as Stiger leaned over him and pulled back his fist to strike. He wanted to beat this man to a bloody pulp. Instead, he hesitated. With not a little bit of effort, he unclenched his fingers, then straightened back up.

"Bind him," Stiger ordered harshly, "and the rest of the prisoners. If any resist, kill them. Oh, and check their right shoulders for a tattoo of a spider. Let me know immediately if you find a man with it."

One of the prisoners lunged for Makaenen's sword. The legionary had been distracted by Stiger's instructions. The auxiliary attempted to wrestle the sword away. Both went down in a tumble, crashing to the floor. Before Stiger could react, Legionary Kencius stabbed the auxiliary in the back. The man stiffened, then rolled over in pain onto his back. The sword strike had taken him in the lung. Blood bubbled up to his lips and out his nose.

"Bastard," Kencius spat as he made a rapid jab to the throat and ended the man's life.

Makaenen pulled himself to his feet, then bent down over the dead auxiliary and tore at the man's tunic.

"He has the mark, sir," Makaenen said.

"He's a follower of Avaya," Stiger said, which was followed by audible gasps and exclamations. The prisoners backed away from the body, as if they might catch the plague, which Stiger thought might not be too far off the mark.

"Drag his body aside and leave it for the paladin to check. Do not touch any of his belongings. No rifling through his clothes for coin. It could be dangerous if he's got anything from Avaya. Understand me?"

"Yes, sir," Makaenen said with a fearful glance thrown to the body.

"And be bloody more careful," Stiger snapped. "I don't want to lose anyone else."

He went to the door and stepped outside, feeling the need for fresh air and to see the stars. The stars would have to wait, for the sky was dark and overcast. It had begun to drizzle. Not too far off, thunder rumbled. Powel, along with several dozen men wearing an assortment of old auxiliary and legionary armor, were forming up in the square. In ones and twos, additional men were streaming in from the darkness, joining those already assembled. There was an elderly priest of the High Father, standing and conversing with Powel. Stiger figured he was Father Senso. Both turned as Stiger slammed the door to the tavern shut. The cold air of the night washed over him.

"It's over," Stiger said to them. "Hanns is dead."

There was a moment of silence.

"Thank the High Father," Powel said, then scowled. "Are you all right, sir? Are you wounded?"

"Have you secured the auxiliary quarters yet?" Stiger asked, ignoring the question.

"I just sent fifty men to do that, sir," Powel said. "I should have a man back shortly with a report."

"Good job," Stiger said. "Send the rest of your men to reinforce the effort at the gate. Have them report to Sergeant Tiro."

"Yes, sir," Powel said. "You look a frightful mess, sir. Have you been injured?"

"If you think I look a mess," Stiger said, untying the straps of his helmet, "you should see Prefect Hanns."

Stiger yanked the helmet off and walked past the militia, Powel, and Senso to the fountain and statue of the High Father. The water tinkled peacefully into the basin. It seemed an odd contrast to the thunder, which rumbled angrily, much closer this time.

Stiger placed his helmet down on the wall that ringed the fountain's basin. He gazed up at the representation of the god he honored and felt a sense of gratefulness for having survived the horror of the underground cavern.

"Thank you, High Father," Stiger said quietly. "Thank you for seeing me through that horror."

There was no answer. He had not expected any. He leaned forward, cupped his hands, and scooped up some water. He splashed the frigid water over his face and began washing the blood and ichor away. Yet again, Eli was right. He most definitely needed a bath.

Chapter Twelve

Stiger sealed the dispatch, then looked up at his two scouts, Bren and Aronus. Both men stood at attention on the opposite side of the table. Stiger had set his headquarters up at the Nag and was using a table in the common room for a desk. It was an hour before dawn on the second day after taking the town. He'd not gotten much sleep. There had been simply too much to do to put things in order and too little time, for he couldn't afford to stay longer in Larensus. He had a mission to complete, gold and a message to deliver to the King of Thresh. General Treim was depending upon him.

He leaned back on his stool, stretching out his back. He glanced down at the dispatch in his hand, considered the contents for a long moment, leaned forward, and handed it across the table to Bren.

"You both go right back to the legion," Stiger said. "As we've discussed, no stopping to jaw with anyone."

"Yes, sir," Bren said. "We'll only stop to camp and, when we do, well away from the road as Eli instructed."

"Right back to the legion," Aronus said. "You can count on us, sir."

"I know I can." Stiger glanced over at Eli, who was leaning against the wall and watching. The elf was silent, his face an inscrutable mask. Eli had not objected to having the scouts he'd been training sent back to the legion, which had been a surprise. Stiger had expected some resistance or at least a counterproposal. Instead, Eli seemed to think it was a good idea or, perhaps more likely, he considered it another test for his scouts.

Stiger and his men owed their lives to Eli. Had he not delivered the warning of the prefect's treachery and intended ambush, they all likely would have been fodder for the worms.

Tiro rested on a stool a few feet away and, like Eli, was silent. The sergeant was in pain but did his best to not let it show. His thigh was heavily bandaged, his injured leg propped on another stool. Father Griggs had examined the wound, a sword cut around four inches in length, and proclaimed it should heal just fine, especially after the local doctor had scrubbed the wound clean with a wool cloth, then liberally poured vinegar all over it before sewing it up. The wound would keep his sergeant sidelined for a few weeks. Tiro would not be going with them to Thresh.

"Use the map I've drawn," Eli said. "Take only those roads and paths I've marked. It should steer you clear of any trouble."

"We will, sir," Bren assured Eli.

"You will still have to be alert," Eli said. "With the majority of the garrison's cohort scattered to the winds, you may happen across a few desperate men."

Stiger's mood darkened. Sergeant Karrax had sent a man back to town to find out why Stiger's men had not marched out as expected. Stiger had the auxiliary brought before him and sent back a simple message.

"Your prefect is dead," Stiger had said. "I now own Larensus and I have the backing of the militia. Surrender and I shall be fair. Run and you will be hunted down like dogs."

Only ten men had turned themselves in. The rest had legged it, along with Karrax. Those ten were now confined with the rest of the prisoners Stiger had taken. Once General Treim received his report, he was certain that all commands for hundreds of miles around would be alerted. Garrisons, militias, and regular units would all be on the lookout for wandering men who were out of place. The fugitives would be hunted down with a vengeance. Desertion and cowardice were bad enough; turning on your own was worse. There was very likely nowhere the fugitives could hide, unless they went north and defected to the Rivan. Even then, they might be killed by the enemy.

Stiger had forty prisoners. Their fate was up to the general. He had no idea what would be done to them. They might face execution, or decimation, the killing of every tenth man. They might even be sold into slavery. Then again, they might be forgiven. The general's need for men was strong, especially after the summer's battles against the Rivan. Stiger put such thoughts from his mind and returned to the matter at hand.

"Stay safe," Stiger said. "Dismissed and good luck."

"Thank you, sir," Bren said as both legionaries saluted. They turned and left the tavern, closing the door behind them.

Stiger was silent for a long moment, staring at the door. He wondered, not for the first time, what the general would make of his report, which had taken hours to write. Stiger picked up his mug of coffee and drained the last of it. Gods, he was tired. The coffee had not helped much.

He stood, pushing his stool back with a foot. He looked over at Tiro, feeling a tinge of regret. He had come to rely upon his sergeant.

"I've asked the general to send a proper surgeon for the wounded," Stiger said.

Five men, including Tiro, had been injured. Two of his men had died in the action. Both had been buried outside of town, along with those auxiliaries killed in the fighting. Father Senso had overseen the funeral arrangements and presided over the ceremony. Stiger was down to eighteen men. He had made the decision to leave eight men behind with Tiro to help care for the wounded and keep the militia and townsfolk from murdering the prisoners in revenge killings.

"I want to be going with you, sir."

"Focus on getting better," Stiger said. "When we get back to the legion, we'll have fresh recruits to train. I'm gonna need you for that."

"Aye, sir," Tiro said. "You can pick me up on your way back from Thresh. I should be back on my feet"—Tiro glanced down at his bandaged thigh—"maybe a little hobbled, but likely able to march by then. I've had worse, sir."

"Your orders." Stiger picked up a wax tablet from the table and handed it over. "It's nothing we've not discussed. You're in charge of the town and militia until the general sees fit to relieve you."

Tiro glanced down at the tablet. "Powel has assured me the locals won't seek vengeance or cause trouble, sir. Father Senso agrees. You should take those eight boys with you. You may need 'em."

"No," Stiger said. "Powel and Senso can say whatever they like. You'll be holding prisoners from the garrison. We both know there are some angry people out there, aggrieved family members and such. You and those eight are a deterrent. The thought of crossing the legion might keep a few hotheads in check, at least long enough for relief to get here. And I expect the general to react quickly. You shouldn't have long to wait."

Tiro looked about to object, then apparently reconsidered. He blew out a breath. "You're likely right, sir. Better safe than sorry."

The door opened. Father Griggs entered. The paladin looked tired, weary even, and moved lethargically. It was as if he'd aged five years over the last two days. After healing Hela, Father Griggs had slept for nearly twenty hours. When he'd awoken, Stiger had asked him if he could heal his injured. Griggs had explained the effort to heal Hela had left him drained. He needed time to recover. It might be weeks before he could perform another healing. The wounded would have to mend the old-fashioned way.

Stiger himself was drained. His recovery would involve leaving Larensus, for the town would always hold dark and disturbing memories. Like those from Fort Covenant, they would be with him for as long as he lived.

"I wish you were coming with us," Stiger said, and in truth he did. He had come to like the paladin.

"My place is here," Griggs said, "at least for the moment. The evil under the tavern must be cleansed, buried, and sealed for all time. Unless dealt with, Avaya's temple will be a terrible temptation for those seeking power, hoping to find powerful artifacts. And we know how that's likely to turn out, don't we?"

Stiger's thoughts drifted back to the horrors below the tavern and the amulet. He'd seen evil beyond imagining and knew he'd never forget. He prayed this would be his last encounter with followers of the dark gods, and not a dark foretoken.

"Did you ask the general for additional men to help me?" Griggs asked. "I'm going to need a lot of labor to do the job properly."

"I did," Stiger confirmed. "My messengers left a short while ago. I expect the general to send nothing less than a company, along with enough supply to stave off famine when winter comes. There should be plenty of men to help you with that effort."

"Thank you," Griggs said.

"I'm sure Father Senso will also be able to mobilize the locals to assist you as well," Stiger said.

"He and I have already spoken about that," Griggs said.

"Good," Stiger said.

The door opened again. Hela entered. It was the first time Stiger had seen her since Griggs had performed his healing. He was relieved to see her well. She hesitated a moment, looking first at Stiger, then Griggs. The paladin gave an encouraging nod. She stepped inside and, with both hands, closed the door behind her. She looked uninjured and whole. Stiger wondered if that extended to her mind. What scars would she carry? What nightmares would she have for the remainder of her days? Having his own, he could well imagine.

Hela's long brown hair had been brushed straight and tied into a tight braid. She wore a wool dress dyed a pale blue. She was an attractive woman and the dress highlighted her fine figure. Stiger felt himself scowl, as he realized she was not wearing appropriate clothing for a slave. She had dressed herself as a freedwoman, which for a slave was against the law. Stiger decided he did not much care. He had more important things to worry about, like getting to Thresh and completing his mission.

Hela stepped up next to the paladin. Her gaze flicked to Eli, then Tiro, lingering upon the bandaged leg a moment, before she lowered her eyes to the floor.

"None of that now, Hela," the paladin chided gently. Griggs reached over and raised her chin with his index finger, drawing her gaze to meet his. "I've given you your manumission. You are a free woman. The High Father has blessed you. Look down no longer, but up."

"Yes, Father," she said in a quiet tone that was almost a whisper. "It may take time, but I swear I shall do it."

Griggs offered her a pleased smile, then turned back to Stiger. "The church will compensate her former master. Father Senso will see to it."

Stiger approved of the paladin's action. After what Hela had been through, he honestly felt she deserved more, but he had nothing to give her. The thought of what had been done to her stirred his anger.

"Captain," Griggs said, "I have a favor to ask before you depart this morning."

"Name it," Stiger said. "If it is within my power, it will be done."

"That's what I thought," Griggs said. "And I believe it is within your power. I would appreciate you taking Hela with you to Haraste."

"Haraste?" Stiger glanced over at Hela. He doubted she would be able to keep up with the pace he intended to set. He had a ship, *The Mars*, waiting for him at the port city, and he'd already been delayed too much as it was.

Surprisingly, Hela held his gaze, and did not look away. Stiger had men in his company who could not do that. He found her eyes haunting and was abruptly reminded of her broken and tortured body in the cavern. It was he who looked away first, turning his attention back to the paladin.

"Why Haraste?"

"There is a temple to Vesta in the city," Griggs continued, "along with a priory of the church. I have written to both the high priestess and the abbot. Hela has letters of introduction. The daughters of Vesta will take Hela in and care for her." He paused, glancing over reassuringly. "Some of my brethren will look in upon her from time to time and help with the healing process." The paladin's gaze returned to Stiger. "Can you accommodate her, Captain? I know the urgency of your mission, but I would take it as a personal favor if she could travel with you. It would bring me great comfort."

"Since I'm only taking ten men, I was planning on leaving a couple of the mules here with Tiro," Stiger said, thinking it through aloud. "I suppose I could spare a mule for her to use as a mount."

"I have a horse," Hela said, the words tumbling out in an excited rush. "Father Griggs was kind enough to give me one. I've always wanted a horse of my own, ever since I was a little girl."

Stiger almost smiled. Her cheeks colored with embarrassment, but she still held his gaze. He found her eyes remarkably deep. She had been through a terrible ordeal, a nightmare beyond imagining. She should be a gibbering wreck but wasn't. She had strength. Hela was a survivor.

"I purchased a mount," Griggs explained. "It's not much, but she should have no trouble keeping up with your pace. I assured her she would have nothing to fear from you and your men."

"Certainly not," Stiger said, harder than he'd intended. Hela flinched slightly. He softened his tone. "We'll see you safely to Haraste."

"Thank you, Captain," Hela said. "You are...quite generous."

"It is the least I can do," Stiger said.

"We will meet you at the town gate in half an hour, Captain," Griggs said.

Stiger gave a nod.

"Come, Hela." Father Griggs took her elbow and guided her toward the door.

Stiger snapped his fingers, remembering something. "Hela?"

She stopped at the door and looked back. Stiger reached beneath his armor and pulled out the necklace with the High Father's eagle attached.

"I believe this belongs to you," Stiger said and set the necklace down on the table.

Her hand went to her mouth as she stared at the silver necklace, eyes watering. She stepped slowly over to the table as if in disbelief and scooped it up. She held the necklace to her chest. "My mother gave this to me. It is all I have left from her. Thank—" She cleared her throat. "Thank you, Captain."

"The chain's snapped, but once we get to Haraste," Stiger said, "I'm sure we can find someone to repair it for you."

"I would like that," Hela said, then turned and stepped out of the tavern with Father Griggs.

Stiger watched them go. Hela was one more problem to worry about, but thankfully only a temporary one. All he had to do was get her to Haraste. He expected no more trouble on his way to the port city. Then again, he'd not thought to find trouble in Larensus.

For some reason, Stiger was reminded of Livia. After his mission to Thresh was over, he was looking forward to spending time with her. Stiger noticed Eli gazing at him, mischief in his eyes, almost as if Eli could read his thoughts. A smart, perhaps even stinging comment was in the making. Instead of waiting for it, Stiger went on the offensive.

"With Bren and Aronus off to the general, are you sure handling the scouting duties won't be too much for you?"

Stiger struggled to keep a grin from his face as Eli's eyebrows rose. "I would not want to overtax you."

Tiro's stool creaked as the sergeant shifted his leg and sat up straighter. It was followed by a heavy moment of silence as Eli just stared at him, long and hard. Stiger loved every bit of it.

"Overtax?" Eli asked, his brow furrowing as he looked over to Tiro in question. "What does overtax mean? I am unfamiliar with the word tax."

"Elves don't use money, sir," Tiro said with a straight face. "You have to dumb it down a bit more if you want them to truly understand."

"Dumb it down?" Eli shot Tiro a scandalized look. "You must be jesting. Dumb it down?"

Something about what Tiro said bothered Stiger slightly.

"If you don't use money," Stiger said, "what do you use then to pay for things?"

"They barter goods and services," Tiro answered. "When it comes to metals, elves only care how one can shape it into things and such. It doesn't have to make much sense to us, but it does to their kind."

"That is more or less true," Eli said. "We have no need for money or the accumulation of wealth, not like you humans." The elf paused and looked back on Tiro with a wounded expression. "After all these years of friendship, you hurt me, Tiro. You truly hurt me to my core. Dumb it down? You well know we elves are your intellectual superiors. I think your age must be getting to you, old man."

"Who are you calling old?" Tiro shot back with a disbelieving chuckle. "An elf calling me old? You're older than the two of us combined. You've likely got more years under your belt than the entire company all added together... well, what's left of it anyway."

"It's not the years that matter, but how you wear them," Eli shot back, then grinned, but said nothing further.

"All right," Stiger said, picking his helmet up off the table. "We've delayed long enough. We've got a long road ahead of us and I want to get started."

Tiro made to stand, struggling up from his stool. Stiger waved his sergeant back down.

"I will see you in a few days," Stiger said. "Take care."

"You too, sir," Tiro said. "Try to stay out of trouble."

"I'm hoping," Eli said, with a sidelong glance over at Stiger, "he sort of finds trouble."

Stiger spared Eli a sour look.

"Knowing you, Eli," Tiro said, "you'll help the captain find some."

"It's more exciting that way," Eli said cheerfully. The elf picked up his pack, which he'd left near the door, along with his bow and a bundle of arrows that had been secured with thin leather straps.

"Larensus hasn't been exciting enough?" Stiger asked, wondering if Eli was serious. "Fort Covenant?"

"It's a start." Eli slipped his pack over a shoulder. "I'll grant it's been somewhat exciting, but you're a Stiger."

"What of it?" Stiger asked, not understanding where the elf was going.

"I expect better from a Stiger."

"Really?" Stiger looked over at Tiro. "You don't think he's serious, do you?"

Tiro did not reply, but instead gave a shrug. Stiger looked back at the elf. Eli shot him a wink.

Stiger barked out a laugh and shook a finger at Eli. "Lepidus said you were going to drive me crazy."

"Sir?"

Stiger looked over at his sergeant.

"I predict you will become fast friends," Tiro said.

"You do?" Stiger asked, with a glance over at Eli. The elf's eyes had narrowed at the sergeant's pronouncement.

"By the gods, I do." Tiro clapped both hands together. "Fast friends, and before you return from Thresh, too."

"Weren't you the one who said Tiro was wise?" Stiger asked Eli, feeling his mood lighten a little.

Eli glanced over at Tiro and then returned his gaze to Stiger. He was silent for several heartbeats. "Whatever happens, I'm still going to drive you crazy."

Stiger grinned broadly, feeling the scar on his cheek pull his skin taut. It felt good to smile. He felt a sudden fondness for the elf. What had begun at Fort Covenant had been sealed by Larensus. Without Stiger even realizing it, Eli had become part of his family, his company. And Tiro was correct. Eli was a friend, someone to be trusted.

"I mean it," Eli said when Stiger did not immediately reply.

"You're welcome to try," Stiger said gamely.

"It will be my mission in life," Eli said.

"See?" Tiro said, beaming. "Best of friends already."

They both looked back on the sergeant.

"Now," Tiro said, and winced as his wound caused him some pain, "just try not to get each other killed, will you? I don't think I could handle losing either of you, not to mention both of you."

"No promises," Stiger said and stepped toward the door, where Eli waited. They regarded each other a moment, then Stiger clapped Eli on the shoulder. "Let's go see Thresh, shall we?"

"It is a place I've long desired to visit." Eli cocked his head to the side. "I wonder what trouble you might get me into there, eh?"

"A nice quiet trip is all I want," Stiger said, "there and back. Is that too much to ask for?"

"We shall see," Eli said. "We shall see."

Stiger shook his head as he opened the door. From across the common room, he saw the kitchen door partially open and Adera poke her head out. She waved. Stiger considered the young girl a moment. Her family was now safe; so were the people of the town and surrounding lands. They no longer had anything to fear from the prefect and his men. Eli was right. They had done a good deed here. He gave Adera a nod, then stepped out into the predawn darkness and cold, where his men were formed up and waiting. He had a mission to complete. Thresh waited.

Epilogue

The oars dug together, the sailors straining with effort, propelling the launch toward the old and decaying dock forty yards away. They rowed silently, pulling in unison, the only sounds being the splash of oars digging at the water and the seabirds calling to one another as they swooped above. The smell of the sea was strong. The stench of the great city, miles away, was masked by the distance.

"We're almost there, sir," the sailor in command of the launch, manning the tiller, said from behind.

Golves did his best not to frown as he turned on his bench and glanced back at the man. He wasn't blind. He could see for himself. Instead, he thanked the sailor, a big brute of a man who was missing most of his teeth. Those few he had left were yellowed and rotting. Golves put the man from his mind and continued to enjoy the sun as the boat drove through the calm waters of the hidden cove, inexorably drawing closer toward the dock. It was the first time he'd seen the sun since they'd set sail a week prior.

He leaned a foot upon the strongbox at his feet. He turned his gaze to the rocky cliffs towering on either side of the small channel as the sailors continued to work the oars. Vegetation, vines, brush, and seagrass grew in patches along the cliff walls, which had been thoroughly weathered by years of harsh winds. Made of gray, chalk-like rock, they were craggy and full of holes.

Golves wished he could have landed at the port and seen the city. It would have been exciting to lay eyes upon the great fortresses guarding the harbor. They were renowned to be some of the most impressive fortifications ever constructed. Instead, the ship's captain had his instructions. Golves was to be put ashore at this little smuggler's cove, hidden and out of view of prying eyes.

The journey by sea had been a miserable, storm-wracked affair. It had been the first time in a great long while Golves had had little to do. His responsibilities were limited to sleeping in his tiny cabin, strolling the rain-lashed deck, and dining with the captain. The latter had not been a pleasant experience, for the ship's captain had been a disagreeable and insufferable fellow.

Captain Meeg was not a gentleman and had no aspirations of becoming one. He'd been born in some gods-forsaken gutter of a port city, somewhere in Castol. The captain had told him, but he'd not cared enough to remember. The captain had led him to believe he and his crew were smugglers, but Golves very much doubted that. The man was likely a pirate and had been paid handsomely to deliver Golves.

Meeg had opinions on everything and expected his passenger to share his views. Golves had on more than one occasion considered killing the man, knifing him over supper, just to enjoy a peaceful meal. He stayed his hand, for the sole reason that he and his men knew nothing about sailing. If he killed the captain, he would have to do the same to the crew, for they seemed absurdly loyal and devoted to the ship's master, especially for slaves. So, he'd kept his thoughts to himself and quietly agreed with the captain's views and allowed the voyage to run its laborious course.

Golves turned. Three additional boats, oars digging at the water, followed along behind his, cutting their way through the cove. They were crowded with his soldiers. Meeg had told him it would take several hours to get his entire company ashore. That bothered Golves little, for where they were headed, friends waited, and he'd been assured there would be no need to worry.

He turned again forward. The voyage had given him plenty of time to stew on his last fight. His company had been part of the failed effort to flank the imperial legions. That had ended in fiasco, where, incredibly, an entire Rivan army had been badly mauled almost to the point of destruction by a single legion. He clenched a fist, the anger returning and almost overcoming him.

His own company had been one of the last to pull out of the assault upon Fort Covenant. When it had come their turn to march, his men had been the rearguard, and as a result, they'd missed much of the battle against Third Legion and the disaster that followed.

Golves still felt the incredible frustration of the defeat. His company was a crack unit and had been obliged to withdraw rather than face certain destruction. He had managed it, just barely, by slipping into the vastness of the forests and away. He felt guilty about running, but in truth the battle had been lost long before he and his men had arrived. Discipline broken and thoroughly whipped by the legionaries, the remains of the Rivan army had disintegrated before his eyes. So, he'd dutifully looked after his own and kept his well-disciplined company together.

In the end, his successful withdrawal had proven a blessing. His company, a unit of the king's own guard, the elite of the Rivan military, was intact. After the remains of the army had come together farther to the north, a small, pitiful remnant of the powerful force that had marched south just weeks before, Golves's company had been pulled out of the line. He had been sent on this sensitive mission.

His new orders had come just in time, for both armies had begun settling into their winter quarters. That had saved Golves from having to endure an uncomfortable winter in field quarters, far from the comforts of civilization. The campaign season, it seemed, had come to an ignominious end, for winter was nearly at hand.

Golves blew out a breath and watched it steam on the cold air. Thinking on Fort Covenant had him once again wondering on the light company he had pursued and hunted over many miles. The officer in command had been a Stiger, one of the empire's nobility. He had proven to be an excellent soldier, eluding Golves until going to ground at Fort Covenant.

Golves had almost gotten Stiger, had even seen and spoken with him. With the fort overrun, the defenders broken, and Stiger almost within reach, the order to withdraw had come. At first, Golves had been stunned and asked for confirmation. He hadn't needed it, for his army had already begun to move, flowing back from the walls of the fort. Those units not engaged had started marching back north, the way they'd come.

He had not known it at the time, but somehow Third Legion had gotten behind the army. The legion had cut the army's communications. That little surprise led to the battle that shattered the Rivan and saw Golves, along with countless others, melt back into the forests.

Golves suppressed his anger and almost sighed with regret. Killing a Stiger would have seen him rewarded, promoted. Still, he did not begrudge the man's escape. Stiger had proven a worthy and cunning adversary. The young

Stiger was now hundreds of miles away, likely killing time in a winter encampment, while Golves had been sent elsewhere on a mission of vast importance to the kingdom.

Perhaps, he thought wistfully, next summer's campaign would see a return to the army. He might even get another shot at this whelp of a Stiger. Perhaps not. The gods were fickle with such things, but one never knew.

"Ship oars," came the call. The oars dutifully went up into the air. The boat coasted alongside the small dock. Several men waited for them. A moment later, the boat bumped into the side of the dock. A man tossed them a rope. A sailor caught it and quickly worked to tie it around a cleat. Golves stood and climbed carefully out of the boat. Stepping onto the dock, he felt extremely pleased to be ashore. He did not much enjoy being at sea.

"Captain Golves, I presume?" one of the waiting men asked. He was wrapped in a finely cut cloak that fluttered slightly in the cold breeze. He had a well-trimmed beard and distinguished features, with a strong jaw and nose. His hair was brown and close-cropped. The man had a cold, almost aloof look to him that spoke of bred superiority.

"Prince Hecklin?" Golves asked, though he already knew the answer. He had a complete description of the ambassador. Only politeness compelled Golves to inquire.

"So good of you to come, my man." The prince held out a hand, palm down. Golves leaned forward, bending his back, and kissed the man's gold ring, his mark and seal of royalty.

"It is an honor to meet you, your highness." Golves felt truly honored, for the ambassador was a prince of his country, related directly to the king. Hecklin was fifth in line of succession. A word one way or the other could see the end of Golves's career, or the making of it.

"How many men did you bring?" the ambassador asked curtly.

"One hundred eighty," Golves replied. "My entire company, your highness."

The prince rubbed his hands together and smiled. "Excellent. Nearly two hundred of the guard. Most excellent."

A chorus of grunting came from behind. Both men turned in time to see the wooden strongbox lifted out of the boat by several sailors and set onto the wooden dock. The strongbox landed with a heavy *thud*.

"Ah." Hecklin smiled broadly. "You brought the gold. We can buy a lot of loyalty with that."

"I would hope so," Golves said. "I've got three more chests just like it."

Hecklin rubbed his hands together in excitement. Golves felt it matched by his own. Together, they would do great work here. If everything went according to plan, Golves would be richly rewarded. War created opportunity and Golves fully intended to cash in. His star was surely on the rise, for they could not fail.

"We have a lot of work to do," Hecklin said. "But, where are my manners? Welcome to Thresh."

The End

Enjoy this short preview of Marc's First book:

Stiger's Tigers:
Chronicles of an Imperial Legionary Officer

Chapter One

Two road-weary riders, both legionary officers, crested the bald hill and pulled to a halt. A vast military encampment surrounded by entrenchments and fortifications took up much of the valley below them in a shocking display. Smoke from thousands of campfires drifted upward and hung over the valley like a veil. After months of travel, the two riders were now finally able to set their eyes upon their destination—the main encampment of General Kromen's Imperial Army, comprising the Fifteenth, Eighteenth, Twenty-Ninth, and Thirtieth Legions. These four legions had been dispatched by the emperor to put down the rebellion burning through what the empire considered her southern provinces.

The awful stench of the encampment had been on the wind for hours. This close, the smell of decay mixed with human waste and a thousand other smells was nearly overpowering. What should have been relief at finally reaching their destination had turned to incredulous horror. Neither of them had ever seen anything like it. Imperial encampments were typically highly organized, with priority placed on sanitation to reduce the chance of sickness and disease. The jumble of tents and ramshackle buildings laid out before them, surrounded by the fortifications, spoke of something much different. It told of an almost wanton criminal neglect for the men who served the empire, or perhaps even incompetence in command.

An empty wagon, the first of a sad-looking supply train, rumbled around past the two riders, who refused to give way. The driver, a hired teamster, cursed at them for hogging the road. He took his frustration out on a group of dirty and ragged slaves sitting along the edge of the road. The slaves, part of a work gang to maintain the imperial highway, were forced to scramble out of the way, lest the wagon roll over them as it rumbled around the two travelers.

An overseer resting on a large fieldstone several feet away barked out a harsh laugh before shouting at the slaves to be more careful. One of the slaves collapsed, and yet both riders hardly spared him a glance. Slaves were simply beneath notice.

The supply train's nominal escort, a small troop of cavalry riding in a line alongside the wagons, was working its way slowly up the hill toward the two officers and away from the encampment. Much like every other legionary the two travelers had come upon for the last hundred miles, the cavalry troop was less than impressive, though somewhat better looking in appearance. Their armor wasn't as rusted and had been recently maintained.

Several empty wagons rumbled by the two, which saw additional invectives hurled their way. They ignored the cursing, just as they had disregarded the wagons and the plight of the slaves. Where they had come from, it would have been unthinkable for someone to hurl invectives at an officer, who was almost assuredly a nobleman. At the very least, a commoner would invite a severe beating with such behavior. Here in the South, such lack of basic respect seemed commonplace.

One of the travelers had the hood of his red imperial cloak pulled up as far as it would go and tilted his head forward to protect against a light drizzling rain, which had been falling for some time.

The other had the hood of his cloak pulled back, revealing close-cropped brown hair and a fair but weather-hardened face, marred only by a slight scar running down the left cheek. The scar pulled the man's mouth up into a slight sneer. He looked no older than twenty-five, but his eyes, which seemed to miss nothing, made him look wise beyond his years. The slaves, having settled down in a new spot, watched the two warily.

As the first of the cavalry troop crested the hill, which was much steeper on the encampment's side, the lieutenant in command pulled his mount up.

"Well met, Captain," the lieutenant said. The lieutenant's lead sergeant also stopped his horse.

The cavalry troop continued to ride by, the men wearing their helmets to avoid the drizzling rain but miserably wet just the same. The lieutenant offered a salute, to which the captain simply nodded in reply, saying nothing. The captain's gaze—along with that of his companion, whose face was concealed by the hood of his cloak—remained focused on the encampment below.

After several uncomfortable moments, the lieutenant once again attempted to strike up a conversation. "I assume you came by way of Aeda? A miserable city, if you ask me. Can you tell me the condition of the road? Did you encounter any rebels?"

The lieutenant shivered slightly as the captain turned a cold gray-eyed gaze upon him.

"We saw no evidence of rebels," the captain replied in a low, gravelly voice filled with steel and confidence. "The road passed peacefully."

"That is good to hear," the cavalry officer replied. "I am Lieutenant Lan of the One Hundred Eighty-Seventh Imperial Horse Regiment. May…may I have your name, Captain?"

"Stiger," the captain growled, kicking his horse into motion and rapidly moving off the crest of the hill, down toward the encampment.

The lieutenant's eyes widened. Stiger's companion, without a word or a sideways glance, followed at a touch to his horse, leaving the lieutenant behind.

The door to the guardhouse opened and after a moment banged closed like it had undoubtedly done countless times before. Stiger and his companion stepped forward, their heavy bootfalls thunking across the coarse wooden floorboards that were covered in a layer of dirt made slick from the rain. The floor had not been swept in a good long time.

"Name and purpose?" a bored ensign demanded, his back to the door. A counter separated the ensign from any newcomers. He was sitting at a table, attempting to look busy and important by writing in a logbook. After a few moments, when the ensign heard nothing in reply, he stood and turned with obvious irritation, prepared to give the new arrivals a piece of his mind. He was confronted with two wet officers, one a captain and the other a lieutenant.

Stiger locked the ensign with a piercing gaze. The ensign was old for his rank, which was generally a sign that he was unfit for further promotion. Instead of forcing such a useless man out of service, he was put in a position where he could do little harm and perhaps accomplish something useful. It had been Stiger's experience that such men became bitter and would not hesitate to abuse what little power was available to them.

Flustered, the ensign tried again. "Name and purp—"

"Captain Stiger and companion," Stiger interrupted, with something akin to an irritated growl. The captain slowly placed his hands on the dirty counter and leaned forward toward the man. The ensign—most likely accustomed to dealing with lowly teamsters, drovers, corporals, and sergeants—blinked. His jaw dropped. He stood there for a moment, dumbfounded, before remembering to salute a superior officer, fist to chest. Stiger said nothing in reply, but gestured impatiently for the ensign to move things along.

"Forgive me, sir," the ensign stammered. It was then, as the lieutenant who accompanied the captain pushed back the hood of his cloak, that he noticed Captain Stiger's companion was not human. The ensign's mouth dropped open even further, if that was possible.

"Lieutenant Eli'Far," the elf introduced himself in a pleasantly soft, singsong kind of voice that sounded human, but was tinged with something alien at the same time. Eli was tall, whipcord thin, and very fair. His perpetually youthful face, complete with blue almond-shaped eyes and sharply pointed ears, was perfect. Framed by sand-colored hair, perhaps it was even *too* perfect.

"I have orders to report to General Kromen," Stiger stated simply, impatient to be done with the fool before him.

"Of course, sir," the ensign stammered, remembering himself. He slid a book across the counter. "If you will sign in, I will have you escorted directly to General Kromen's headquarters."

Stiger grabbed a quill, dipped it in the inkbottle sitting on the counter, and signed for both himself and Eli. He put down the quill and pushed the book back toward the ensign.

"Corporal!" the ensign called in a near-panicked shout.

The guard corporal poked his head into the guardhouse. "Captain Stiger requires an escort to the commanding general's headquarters."

The corporal blinked as if he had not heard correctly. "Yes, sir," he said, fully stepping into the guardhouse, eyes wide. "This way, gentlemen," the corporal said in a respectful tone. It was never wise to upset an officer, and even more irresponsible to offend one from an important family, no matter how infamous. "I will escort you myself. It is a bit of a ride, sirs."

The two traveling companions followed the corporal out of the guardhouse. They stepped back into the rain, which had changed from a drizzle to a steady downpour. Eli pulled his hood back up, once again obscuring his features. Stiger left his down. They retrieved their horses from where they had secured them and mounted up. The corporal also mounted a horse that was waiting for such a purpose and led them through the massive wooden gate that served as the encampment's main entrance. Stiger was disgusted to see the sentries huddled for cover under the gate's overhang. Those men should have been on post despite the weather.

Stiger had thought it impossible for the stench of the encampment to get any worse, yet it became much more awful and unpleasant once they were clear of the gate. It made his eyes burn. He had only ever once encountered a worse smell. That had been years before on a distant battlefield, with the dead numbering in the many thousands under a brutally hot sun, rotting quicker than they could be buried or burned.

Massive numbers of tents and temporary ramshackle wooden buildings spread out before them, amongst a sea of mud flowing with animal and human excrement. The three worked their way slowly through the muddy streets with rows of tents on each side. They came upon a small stream, muddy brown and swollen from the day's rain, running through the center of the encampment. The stream was threatening to flood nearby tents.

A rickety wooden bridge, which looked as though it had been hastily constructed to ford the small stream, appeared at risk of being washed away by the growing rush of water. Unconcerned, the corporal guided them over the bridge and to a large rough-looking building directly in the center of the encampment. An overhang and porch had been constructed onto the building, almost as an afterthought, but probably in response to the rain and mud.

Several staff officers on the porch loitered about in chairs, idly chatting and smoking pipes or playing cards, as the three horsemen approached. It was clear this was the main headquarters. A rough planked boardwalk that looked like it might sink into the mud at any moment connected the building to a row of larger tents and other nearby buildings. The porch and boardwalk served the purpose of saving the officers from having to get their perfectly polished boots muddy.

A dirty and ragged slave, ankles disappearing in the muck, stepped forward to take the reins of their horses as the two officers dismounted. Stiger tried to avoid thinking about what was in the mud as his boots sank into it.

"Good day, sirs." The corporal saluted and swung his horse around, riding away before anything more could be required of him. Stiger understood that the man was relieved to be on his way. It was said that bad things tended to happen around Stigers.

"This camp is an embarrassment," Eli said quietly to Stiger. "It is very unfit."

"I hazard half the camp is down sick," Stiger responded in sour agreement. He had never seen a legionary encampment in such a state. "Let us hope we are not detained here for months on end."

The two walked through the mud and up the steps to the front porch of the headquarters building, where they hastily kicked and scraped the muck from their boots. The headquarters building was not at all what one would expect for the commanding general of the South. The finely attired officers on the porch purposefully ignored the new arrivals. Stiger hesitated a moment and then stepped toward the building's entrance, reaching for the door.

"Where exactly do you think you're going?" a young staff captain sitting in a chair demanded disdainfully without looking up from his card game. The man was casually smoking and took a rather slow pull from his pipe, as if to show he was in charge.

Stiger turned to look at the staff captain, who wore expensively crafted legionary officer armor over a well-cut tunic and rich black boots. The armor was highly polished and the fine red cloak appeared to be freshly cleaned and brushed. There was not a hint of mud or dirt anywhere on the officer. He almost looked like the perfect toy soldier. Stiger took him to be of the soft type, a spoiled and pampered nobleman, likely from a minor yet wealthy house. At least wealthy or influential enough to secure his current position. Much like the ensign in the guardhouse, Stiger had also unfortunately encountered this kind of officer before—a bootlicking fool. Stiger's lip curled ever so slightly in derision. The bootlicker, more concerned with his fawning entourage of fellow officers, did not seem to notice. Eli, however, did. He placed a cautioning hand on Stiger's arm, which had come to rest upon the pommel of his sword.

"I am ordered to report to General Kromen and that is what I intend to do," Stiger responded neutrally, casually pulling his arm away from Eli's restraining hand. The elf sighed softly. "Unless, of course, the general is not present. In that event I shall simply wait for his return."

"Oh, I believe the general is in," the captain said with a sneer. "However, you do not get to see him without my personal permission."

Several of the other officers snickered.

"Perhaps you should say... please?" one of the other officers suggested with a high-pitched voice. The others openly laughed at this.

Stiger's anger flared, though he kept the irritation from his face. The captain was likely an aide to the general, a player of camp politics, working to control access and thereby strengthening his powerbase. He was the kind of man who was rarely challenged openly. He was also someone who would most definitely hold a grudge if he was ever slighted or offended. In short, he was another arrogant fool, and Stiger loathed such men.

Suffer the fool's game or not? Stiger was new to the camp and the last thing he wanted was to get off on the wrong foot. Still, the captain's manner irritated him deeply. The man should have behaved as a gentleman, and yet he had blatantly offended Stiger. Should he continue, Stiger would be justified in issuing a challenge to satisfy honor. Somehow, Stiger doubted General Kromen would approve of him killing, or at best maiming, one of his staff officers on his first day in camp.

"Stop me," Stiger growled. He opened the door and stepped through. The staff captain scrambled out of his chair and gave chase, protesting loudly.

Inside, Stiger was greeted by a nearly bare room. The interior was intentionally darkened, the windows shuttered. Several lanterns provided moderately adequate lighting. A fireplace, set along the back wall, crackled. The chimney, poorly constructed, leaked too much smoke into the building. A table with a large map spread out on it dominated the center of the room. Three men stood around the table, while another, a grossly obese man, sat in a chair with his elbows resting heavily on the tabletop. He had the look of someone who was seriously ill. His face was pale and covered in a sheet of fever sweat. They all looked up at the sudden intrusion, clearly irritated. Two were generals, including the one who was seated, and the two others held the rank of colonel.

"What is the meaning of this intrusion?" the general who was standing demanded. He had a tough, no-nonsense look about him.

"I am sorry, sir," the bootlicking staff captain apologized, pushing roughly past Stiger and Eli. "I tried to stop them."

"Well?" the general demanded again of Stiger.

Unfazed by the rank of the men in the room, Stiger pulled his orders from a side pocket in his cloak and stepped forward. "I am ordered to report to General Kromen for duty."

"I am General Kromen," the large, seated man wheezed before being consumed by a wracking cough. After a few moments he recovered. "Who in the seven levels might you be?"

"Captain Stiger reporting for duty, sir." Stiger assumed a position of attention and saluted.

"A Stiger?" the staff captain whispered, taking a step back in shock.

The other general barked out a sudden laugh, while General Kromen went into another coughing fit that wracked his fat body terribly.

"Captain Handi," General Kromen wheezed upon recovering, waving a hand dismissively. His other hand held a handkerchief to his mouth. "It would seem," he coughed, "we have important matters to discuss. You may go."

The captain hesitated a moment, looking between the standing no-nonsense general and the seated one before saluting smartly. He left the room without saying another word, though he managed to shoot a hate-filled look at Stiger as he passed.

"A Stiger!" Kromen exclaimed in irritation once the door was closed. "Who is your companion?"

Eli reached up and pulled back his hood, showing his face for the first time.

"Hah!" Kromen huffed tiredly. "An elf. I swear, I never thought I'd see one of your kind again, at least in this life."

"Sadly, we are few in these lands, General," Eli responded neutrally, with a slight bow.

"An elf, as well as imperial officer? I thought you fellows had given up on the empire," the other general stated.

"The emperor granted a special dispensation to serve the one known here as Ben Stiger," Eli answered, nodding in the direction of the captain. The nod had an odd tilt to it that reminded everyone present he was not quite human. Human necks just did not bend like that. "The rank conferred was to help me better serve."

"You serve a human?" the standing general asked with some surprise before turning back to Stiger. "What did you do to earn that dubious honor, Stiger?"

"I, ah ..." Stiger began after a slight hesitation, "would prefer not to discuss it, sir."

"The emperor," Kromen breathed with a heavy sigh, steering the conversation away from a direction that Stiger was clearly uncomfortable speaking on. "The emperor and the gods have forsaken us in this wicked and vile land."

Kromen was an old and wily politician. Stiger suspected that the general would not press him, but would instead write back to his family in the capital to get an answer. Information was often more important than the might of an entire legion. More importantly, Stiger knew that Kromen wanted to know why a Stiger, a member of one of the most powerful families in the empire, was here in the South, and that required moving the conversation along.

"Perhaps not...You asked for combat-experienced officers and men of quality. Well...here stands a Stiger," the other general said after a moment's reflection, taking General Kromen's subtle nudge to change the subject. Stepping over, he took Stiger's orders. "Were you in the North?"

"Emperor's Third Legion," Stiger replied.

"The Third gets all of the shit assignments." The general handed the orders over to General Kromen, who opened them and began reviewing the contents. Silence filled the room, and all that could be heard was the pop of the logs in the fireplace and the rustle of parchment as General Kromen read.

"An introduction letter from my good friend General Treim," Kromen breathed hoarsely as he read.

Stiger was familiar with the contents of the letter. According to the letter, the emperor had directed Treim to send a few of his best and most promising officers to the South. Stiger could imagine Kromen's thoughts as the general looked up briefly with a skeptical look. The general was finding it hard to imagine that Treim would release one of his truly outstanding officers. The politician in Kromen would scream that there was more here than met the eye. Perhaps even the general might consider this whelp of a Stiger was actually a spy for his enemies in the senate looking to gain some advantage. Though the Kromen and Stiger families were not actually enemies, they were not allies either.

"Interesting," Kromen said after a few silent minutes, and then turned to the other general. "General Mammot, it seems that our good friend General Treim has dispatched this officer at *our* request. The letter indicates more such officers of quality are on the way. Interesting, don't you think?"

"Very," General Mammot replied dryly. "How long did it take you to travel down here, Stiger?"

"Three and a half months, sir."

General Kromen was consumed by another fit of coughing. He held a handkerchief to his mouth, hacking into it.

"Impressive time," General Mammot admitted with a raised eyebrow and turned to Kromen. "Do you think he can fight?"

"General Treim," cough, "seems to think so." Kromen handed over the letter of introduction, which General Mammot began reading. After a moment, he stopped and looked up, a strange expression crossing his face.

"You volunteered and led not one, but two forlorn hopes?" Mammot asked in an incredulous tone. "Do you have a death wish, son?"

Stiger elected not to respond and remained silent. Mammot continued to read.

"Seems General Treim sent us a fighter, and the elf comes as a bonus." Kromen took a deep and labored breath, having somewhat recovered from his latest coughing fit. He seemed to make a decision. He looked over meaningfully at General Mammot, who paused in his reading and caught his look. "We were discussing a pressing issue..."

"We were," Mammot agreed.

"Well then... since we are now saddled with a... Stiger, perhaps he might prove of some assistance in resolving this irritating matter with Vrell? Don't you agree?"

General Mammot frowned slightly and considered Stiger for a moment before nodding in agreement. He waved both Stiger and Eli over to the table with the map.

"Stiger," Mammot said, "allow me to introduce Colonels Karol and Edin. They are brigade commanders from the Twenty-Ninth."

"Pleased to meet you, Stiger," Colonel Karol said, warmly offering his hand. "I fought with your father when I was a junior officer. How is the old boy?"

"Well, sir," Stiger replied. His father was a touchy subject with most other officers. He found it was best to be vague in his answers to their questions. "His forced retirement wears on him."

"I can understand that," Colonel Karol said. "Perhaps one day he may be permitted to once again take the field."

"I am not sure he ever will," Stiger replied carefully. Many would feel threatened by such sentiments.

Colonel Edin simply shook hands and refrained from saying anything. Stiger could read the disapproval in the man's eyes. It was something the captain had grown accustomed to from his fellow officers.

"Now that we are all acquainted," General Mammot began, directing everyone's attention to the map on the table, "we have an outpost four weeks' march from here, located at Vrell, an isolated valley to the east with a substantial population." Mammot traced a line along a road from the encampment to the outpost for Stiger to follow. "Specifically, the outpost garrisons one of the few castles in the South. We call it Castle Vrell. The locals call it something different."

"We have not heard from them for several weeks," Kromen rasped. "We have dispatched messengers, but none have returned. It is all very irritating."

"The castle is a highly fortified position," Mammot continued. "There are over nine hundred legionaries defending it and the valley. Vrell is an out-of-the-way place, surrounded by mountains and a nearly impenetrable forest. We think the castle unlikely to have fallen to enemy forces." With his hand, Mammot traced a new line on the map, well south of Vrell. "The rebels control everything south of this line here... There are no roads traveling to rebel territory from Vrell. Beyond the mountains, it is all thick forest for about one hundred miles to rebel territory. The only road to Vrell moves from the encampment here, eastward, through the Sentinel Forest and terminates at the valley. It is our opinion the enemy has simply cut our communications with a handful of irregulars."

"The garrison commandant, Captain Aveeno, has been complaining for months of rebels harassing his patrols and stirring up trouble," Colonel Karol spoke up. "Then suddenly, nothing... no word."

"The garrison is due for resupply," Kromen added, taking another labored breath. "Normally we would send a simple cavalry escort. However, with the road apparently infested with rebel irregulars, a foot company appears to be the more sensible approach."

"The Third has been heavily involved up north in the forests of Abath," General Mammot said. "We would appreciate your expertise on the matter."

"Sounds like a difficult assignment," Stiger said, non-committally. "How are the rebels equipped in this area?"

"Poorly." Colonel Edin spoke for the first time. "This terrain presents a very difficult obstacle for the rebels to overcome. We have only ever encountered light units, mostly conscripted farmers... the equivalent of bandits."

"What is the condition of the road?" Stiger leaned forward to study the map more closely. Eli stepped closer as well. The map was a simple camp scribe copy.

"Poor, but passable for wagons," Karol admitted. "Imperial maintenance crews repaired it just three years ago, so there should be no significant problems for the supply train."

"I don't see any towns and villages." Stiger found that odd for such a long road.

"There are—or were—a handful of what you might call farming communities," Edin admitted. "Really the remnants. I personally would be surprised if you discovered anyone left."

"Reprisals?" Stiger asked, looking up at Edin. He already knew the answer.

"That was my predecessor's work," General Kromen answered carefully. "A nasty business, though he did a good job in clearing the bastards out. There should be no one left to support the rebels, at least we think, until you get to Vrell. The valley's population is not with the rebels. For some strange reason, they seem to think of themselves as imperials, or at least descended from imperial stock. That said, they are not exactly friendly, at least according to Captain Aveeno's last reports."

"Captain Aveeno could have sent a force to break through, could he not?" Stiger asked.

"Not very likely," Mammot answered with a heavy breath. "Captain Aveeno, the garrison commandant, is a bit cautious. He likely would have put everyone on short rations and kept them in defense of the castle and valley, rather than take the risk of losing additional men."

"Aveeno comes from a good family," General Kromen wheezed, speaking up in defense of the man. "However, he is a timid sort, which is why he is commanding a garrison instead of leading a line company."

Stiger nodded, understanding what had not been said. General Kromen was likely Aveeno's patron, hence his defense. "A good company should be able to get through, then," Stiger said, looking down at the map once again. "Should the rebel forces operating in the area prove superior, a company will likely be able to get word out or at least fight its way back."

"Excellent," Kromen said, looking from Eli to Stiger. "How would you like the job? I have an absolutely terrible company that just became available. With your experience, you are perfect for working it into shape!"

Stiger was surprised he was being given a mission that would take him away so soon after arriving. Though marching with unfamiliar men into territory overrun by rebels was not a terribly appealing idea to the captain, his initial impressions of the legionary encampment led him to believe that such a march would be preferable to risking an untimely death by lingering sickness. He knew that the command he was being offered was most probably, as the general said, a truly terrible assignment. If the men had been idle for months, as he suspected they had, they would be sick, poorly equipped, and out of shape, and discipline would be lacking. So it all came down to risking potential death from slow, lingering sickness and disease or possible death by sword... Stiger intentionally drew out the silence, as if he were mulling it over. Surely there were other, more effective companies that could be more readily chosen. The two generals, he knew, were also making light of the assignment so that it seemed too easy... too good. That bothered Stiger, and he wanted to know why, but could not come right out and ask.

"I would need to outfit the company for a hard march into the wilderness," Stiger said.

"You can draw anything you might require from supply," Kromen responded, almost a little too quickly, which surprised Stiger.

What wasn't he being told?

Stiger had known that his arrival might be a headache for General Kromen. Stiger's family had influence. His presence here might be viewed as the attempt to place a spy within the Southern legions, a spy who was possibly reporting directly to the emperor or Kromen's enemies in the senate.

"We need to open communications with Vrell," Mammot added. "We can issue your company fresh arms and equipment. I will also assign some of our most experienced sergeants to help you work them into fighting trim."

"Could I meet and approve the sergeants first?" Stiger asked. He had known some pretty terrible sergeants, from ass-kissers to sadistic bastards. Instead of being dismissed from the service, such men were frequently transferred from one unit to another.

"Of course," Kromen said.

"How long until the supply train is ready?" Stiger asked, thinking about the training of his men. He needed time to become acquainted with them and to work them into shape. All legionaries received the same basic training. It was a matter of restoring discipline and finding out how rusty they had become.

"Two weeks," Mammot said. "At least, we hope the train will arrive within two weeks, but certainly no more than four. It is due to leave from Aeda any day."

"Good, that would give me some time," Stiger said. He looked at General Kromen, thinking hard. "I would want to train the men my way, with no outside interference."

"Acceptable," General Kromen said with a deep frown. No general enjoyed being dictated to, especially by a young, impudent captain, even if he was a Stiger. Still…Kromen seemed to put up with it, and Stiger decided to push for more.

"That would involve training outside the encampment and living beyond the walls," Stiger added. "I would need space to prepare the men…construction of a marching camp, route marches, arms training…"

"If you are willing to brave a rebel attack outside the protection of the walls, you can do whatever you flaming wish," Kromen said, his dangerous tone betraying a mounting anger. "Anything else you require, captain?"

"No, sir," Stiger said, pleased at having escaped the confines of the encampment so easily. In all likelihood, whatever he had been set up for would prove to be a real challenge. "I will take the job."

"Very good." General Kromen flashed an insincere smile. "Colonel Karol will arrange to have you introduced to your men. He will also see to outfitting your needs." Kromen waved dismissively, indicating the audience was over.

Stiger saluted along with Colonel Karol. They turned and left, emerging onto the porch with Eli in tow. Stiger found Captain Handi resting in the same chair. The captain shot Stiger a look that spoke volumes. Doubtless Handi would be looking for ways to get his petty revenge. Stiger simply ignored him.

"You have a tough job ahead of you," Karol admitted. "The men I am giving you are in truly terrible shape and have been poorly led. Their previous commander was executed for gross incompetence. His real crime, however, was excessive graft and insufficient… shall we say, *sharing*."

"I have always enjoyed a challenge," Stiger replied softly.

"Let us both hope this particular challenge does not kill you," Karol responded. The colonel glanced to the side at the lounging officers toward Handi, who was aiming a smoldering glare at Stiger. "Captain Handi, be so good as to personally fetch Sergeants Blake and Ranl. They should be working over at my headquarters."

"But, sir, it's raining," Handi protested, gesturing at the steady rainfall beyond the cover of the porch.

"I rather imagine that the emperor expects his legions to operate in all types of weather," the colonel responded rather blandly. "Have them report on the double to the officers' mess."

Colonel Karol turned away and stepped out into the rain. He led them along the improvised boardwalk system toward another smaller ramshackle wooden building with a chimney billowing with soft blue-gray smoke.

"Wouldn't want that spoiled bastard to get his fine boots muddy now, would we?" Karol asked once they were out of earshot. Stiger found himself beginning to like the colonel.

A Note from the Author

I want to thank you for reading my latest book. I sincerely hope you enjoyed it. Writing a book like this takes a tremendous amount of time, effort, and energy. A review would be awesome and greatly appreciated.

The original name of this book was entitled *Eli*. Though Eli plays a strong role in this book, I made the decision to change the name, as I want to save the title *Eli* for a later, more pivotal book in this series. *A Dark Foretoken*, I think is a more fitting name for this story.

Tales of the Seventh began as an experiment…a way to give readers more Stiger while they waited for the Chronicles books. Released one chapter at a time for free on my website under the title of *The Interludes*, it was meant only to be a novella, but Part One quickly grew into a full-blown novel. It was an instant hit, with readers messaging me on Facebook and emailing questions and thoughts on what would happen next. (Please note: This final version is slightly different than the original and more polished.)

I fully intend to continue writing Tales of the Seventh books. They will always be on the shorter side and designed to be quick reads that will fill in Stiger and Eli's rich backstory.

Important: If you have not yet given my other series—Chronicles of an Imperial Legionary officer, or The Karus Sage—a shot, I strongly recommend you do. All of my series are linked and set in the same universe. There are hints, clues, and Easter eggs sprinkled throughout.

The Series:
There are three series to consider. I began telling Stiger and Eli's story in the middle years…starting with Stiger's Tigers, published in 2015. *Stiger's Tigers* is a great place to start reading. It was the first work I published and is a grand fantasy epic.

Stiger, Tales of the Seventh, covers Stiger's early years. It begins with Stiger's first military appointment as a wet-behind-the-ears lieutenant serving in Seventh Company during the very beginning of the war against the Rivan on the frontier. This series sees Stiger cut his teeth and develop into the hard-charging leader that readers have grown to love. It also introduces Eli and covers many of their early adventures. These tales should in no way spoil your experience with *Stiger's Tigers*. In fact, I believe they will only enhance it.

The Karus Saga is a whole new adventure set in the same universe…many years before Stiger was even born. This series tells how Roman legionaries made their way to the world of Istros and the founding of the empire. It is set amidst a war of the gods and is full of action, intrigue, adventure, and mystery.

Give them a shot and hit me up on Facebook to let me know what you think!

Best regards and again thank you for reading! -Marc

Join Marc's Newsletter

Stay up to date! Care to be notified when the next book is released and receive updates from the author? Join the mailing list! You can find it on Marc's website:

http://www.MAEnovels.com
Facebook: Marc Edelheit Author
https://www.facebook.com/MAENovels/

Printed in Poland
by Amazon Fulfillment
Poland Sp. z o.o., Wrocław